THE SONS OF
DANIEL SHAYE

VENGEANCE CREEK

ROBERT J. RANDISI

HarperTorch
An Imprint of HarperCollinsPublishers

This is a work of fiction. Names, characters, places, and incidents are products of the author's imagination or are used fictitiously and are not to be construed as real. Any resemblance to actual events, locales, organizations, or persons, living or dead, is entirely coincidental.

❧

HARPERTORCH
An Imprint of HarperCollins*Publishers*
10 East 53rd Street
New York, New York 10022-5299

Copyright © 2005 by Robert J. Randisi
ISBN 0-06-058348-7

All rights reserved. No part of this book may be used or reproduced in any manner whatsoever without written permission, except in the case of brief quotations embodied in critical articles and reviews. For information address HarperTorch, an imprint of HarperCollins Publishers.

First HarperTorch paperback printing: March 2005

HarperCollins ®, HarperTorch™, and ❧™ are trademarks of Harper-Collins Publishers Inc.

Printed in the United States of America

Visit HarperTorch on the World Wide Web at www.harpercollins.com

10 9 8 7 6 5 4 3 2 1

If you purchased this book without a cover, you should be aware that this book is stolen property. It was reported as "unsold and destroyed" to the publisher, and neither the author nor the publisher has received any payment for this "stripped book."

To Ford Fargo,
in appreciation of his good humor
and cooperative spirit.

VENGEANCE CREEK

PROLOGUE

Three dead sons.

Just the thought caused Dan Shaye more pain than he felt he could endure—if it turned out to be true.

He'd already lost one son, and his wife, and it had only been a year. He'd barely survived the deaths of Matthew and Mary. If he lost Thomas and James as well, there'd be nothing left for him to live for.

He'd crossed into Colorado several days ago. The trail he was following was barely there. Luckily, he was as good a reader of sign as he had ever met. As long as there was a ghost of a trail, he'd be able to follow it. As long as there was a ghost of a trail, there was a chance he'd find his sons, alive and well.

He filled his canteen from the waterhole he'd camped next to and walked back to his horse. He'd already stomped out his campfire and stored his supplies back in his saddlebags. Traveling light, all he'd had for dinner and for breakfast had been coffee and beef jerky. He didn't figure he deserved much more than that.

He never should have let them go. They weren't experienced enough. He mounted up and sat there for a moment, head bowed. He was almost glad their mother was dead, just so he wouldn't have to tell her how he had gotten their sons killed—all three sons.

1

Daniel Shaye wasn't all that sure how he and his sons had come to settle in Vengeance Creek, Arizona. Maybe the name had appealed to them. After the Langer gang had robbed the bank in Epitaph, Texas—killing Shaye's wife, the boys' mother, during their escape—they had hunted them down and extracted their vengeance at a heavy cost. The man who had ridden his wife down with a horse had paid with his life, but not before he'd killed another member of the family, Shaye's middle son, Matthew. Vengeance had cost them dearly, so maybe it made sense that they settled some months later in Vengeance Creek.

That had been over a year ago, and now Shaye was the sheriff of Vengeance and his two sons were his deputies. Odd how things happened. Shaye had left his job as sheriff of Epitaph behind, feeling that it had, in part, contributed to the deaths of his wife and son. Arriving in Vengeance Creek penniless and looking for work, he found that the lawman job was open. There had been no election because no one else wanted to run for the office. No one wanted the job. Vengeance Creek had a rowdy populace, and most of them liked the idea of having no lawman.

Shaye recalled discussing the situation with his sons.

"You want to pin on a badge again, Pa?" Thomas had asked. At twenty-six, he was the older of the two remaining sons.

"The way I see it," Shaye had said, "we've got three options, given the skills we have to work with. We can hunt bounty, take up the owl-hoot trail . . . or pin on badges again."

"Badges?" James, nineteen, asked. "You mean us too?"

"Well," Shaye said, "if I'm the sheriff, you two will be my deputies. We'll present ourselves to the town council as a package deal. Whataya say, boys?"

Thomas and James exchanged a glance, and then Thomas said, "Why not? What have we got to lose?"

Shaye made his presentation to the town council, and they went for it. He became sheriff, and his two sons became his deputies.

Now, roughly nine months after pinning on the badges for the first time, there was some law and order in town. The "rowdy" element had either straightened up or left. It seemed Shaye's Texas reputation had preceded him, and after he and his boys had handled the first few altercations, the people got the message: You don't step over the line in Dan Shaye's town.

Shaye wondered what the people would think if they knew that in his youth he'd been a gunman named Shaye Daniels, with a reputation in Missouri, Kansas, and the Indian Territory. It was more than likely they wouldn't even recognize the name. But his rep as a lawman—well, that had spread since the word got out that he hunted down not one, but both Langer brothers, and their whole gang.

Shaye got up from his desk and walked over to the window. He looked out at Vengeance Creek's main street. His boys were out there, making their rounds. Had it been the right thing to do, making them pin badges on again? It had actually been Thomas who killed Ethan Langer, taking revenge for his mother's and brother's deaths. Shaye could see the changes in Thomas, changes that killing another man couldn't help but make. James had changed too.

In fact, they'd all changed since leaving Epitaph to hunt down the Langers, and then leaving again, for good. Maybe, he thought, he should have allowed the boys to make up their own minds about what they wanted to do. Oh, he'd given them a choice, but they knew he wanted them to take this job with him, and they would have died before disappointing him. Perhaps it was time, now, to give them the push to make their own choices about their lives.

Then again, as a young man he'd made his own choice, and it had been the wrong one. Maybe if he'd had the strong hand of a father in his life, it would have been different. But both of his parents had died of a fever, leaving him to make his own way. His boys had lost their mother, but they still had a father around to help them.

It was coming up on a year since their mother and brother had been killed. Maybe it was time to sit down and have a family meeting. They were, after all, men, and men deserved the leeway to make up their own minds. . . .

In another part of town, Thomas and James Shaye were peering into the bank through the front window. Well, James was looking inside. Thomas's eyes were sweeping the street, watching for trouble.

"There she is," James said suddenly.

"James, if you like this girl so much why don't you go in and talk to her?"

"I have talked to her."

"When?"

"Just yesterday."

"You mean when you made a deposit?" Thomas asked. "What did you say, 'please' and 'thank you'?"

James turned to look at his big brother. "I don't want to rush into anything, Thomas."

"Because you're scared?"

"No," James said patiently, "because I don't want to scare her."

Thomas took a moment to lean down and look into the bank through the window. "Which one is she?"

"The blonde."

"The skinny one?"

"She's not skinny," James said defensively. "She's just . . . kind of slender."

Thomas straightened and looked at his brother. "Well, she's a little too skinny for me. Come on, we've got to finish our rounds."

Thomas started walking away, while James took one more peek through the window at Jenny Miller, his favorite bank teller, and then hurried to catch up.

Vengeance Creek had appealed to both of them because it was roughly the same size as Epitaph. During the hunt for the Langers, they'd been through small towns and larger places, like Oklahoma City, but both Thomas and James preferred something in between, a place not very small, with some growing left to do.

Lately, however, Thomas had been growing restless. He knew he'd changed since killing Ethan Langer, but he wasn't all that sure how. He only knew that of late he'd been thinking of those nights on the trail with his father and his brothers. He'd learned a lot from his father during the months they'd been hunting the Langers. They all had. But it seemed to him it was all going to waste just being a deputy in a town like Vengeance Creek.

James was not quite as restless as his brother. He'd settled in a bit more, had made a few friends, and had spotted a girl he liked. But he was young—barely twenty—and none of those things appealed to Thomas very much.

"It's a year, you know," James said.

"What?"

"A year," the younger brother said, "since Ma and Matthew . . . you know."

"Yes," Thomas said, "I know."

"I miss them both."

"I do too."

James looked at Thomas quickly. "You do? Really?"

"Of course," Thomas said, "whataya think, James?"

"Well . . . you never say anything," James replied. "You never mention them."

"Just because I never mention them doesn't mean I don't miss them."

"Think Pa knows?" James asked. "That it's been a year, I mean?"

"He knows, James," Thomas said, putting his arm around his brother's shoulder. "He always knows exactly how long it's been."

Thomas and James finished their rounds in time for supper, and Shaye took them over to the Carver House Café for steaks and conversation.

It was dinnertime, but the Carver House kept a table open for Shaye and his deputies at all times. On the way to their table they exchanged nods with the mayor and several members of the town council and their families.

"You know what I notice?" James asked as they sat down.

"What, James?" Shaye asked.

"Nobody ever asks you to eat with them, Pa," the younger Shaye said. "Not since we first came to this town."

"Why should they do that, son?" Shaye asked. "We aren't friends with these people, we just work for them."

"You had a lot of friends in Epitaph, Pa," James argued.

"A lot of good that did your mother a year ago

in the street," Shaye said. "I know you boys haven't forgotten what today is."

"No, Pa," Thomas said, giving his brother a hard look. "We remember."

"Stop looking at your brother that way, Thomas."

"I'm sorry for bringin' it up, Pa," James said, putting his head down.

"Nothing to be sorry for, son," Shaye said. "You boys have got minds of your own. That's kinda what I wanted to talk to you about tonight."

At that point the waiter came and Shaye ordered steak dinners for the three of them.

"Burn 'em," he told the waiter, who already knew that.

"Pa," Thomas said, "if we got minds of our own, I'd kinda like to have mine rare . . . if that's okay?"

"That's fine, Thomas," Shaye said. To the waiter, he added, "Burn two of 'em and make one rare . . . unless . . ." He paused to look at James.

"Burnt is fine with me, Pa," he said.

Shaye looked at the waiter and nodded.

"Comin' up, Sheriff."

"Thomas," Shaye asked as the waiter moved off, "how long you been eating your steaks rare?"

"Uh, whenever I'm not with you, Pa."

"Boy," Shaye said, "you eat your steaks however you please, you hear?"

"Yes, sir."

"And that goes for you too, James."

"Yes, Pa."

The waiter came back with three mugs of beer, which the three men hadn't even had to ask for.

"Beer okay, Thomas?" Shaye asked, picking his up. "You haven't gone and acquired a taste for whiskey, have you?"

"No, Pa," Thomas said. "Beer's fine."

"Me too, Pa."

"You better not be drinking whiskey, young man," Shaye said to James. "You're barely twenty."

"I'm a man full growed, Pa."

Shaye hesitated, then took a gulp of beer before speaking.

"That you are, James," he said. "You both proved that to me last year. So, James, I guess if you want to drink whiskey—"

"I don't, Pa," James said. "It burns too much going down."

Shaye laughed. "You get a little older, son, you're gonna learn to like that burn."

"What was it you wanted to talk to us about, Pa?" Thomas asked.

"You boys have been good sons, and good deputies," Shaye said, "but I think it's time for you to choose for yourselves."

"I really do like my steak rare, Pa," James insisted.

"I'm talking about your lives, James," Shaye said, "not your steaks."

"Whataya mean, Pa?" Thomas asked.

"I mean you don't have to be lawmen if you don't wanna be," Shaye said. "If you boys want to take off your badges, or even move on, I'll understand."

"Move on?" Thomas repeated.

"You—You want us to leave, Pa?" James asked.

"Only if you want to," Shaye said hurriedly. "I'm not trying to chase you boys away. I just want you to know that I realize that you're men, and that you have your own lives."

"I don't know about James, Pa," Thomas said, "but I don't want to go anywhere. I want to stay here and be your deputy. And maybe, someday, when I've learned all that you can teach me, I can become a sheriff myself."

Shaye reached out and touched his son's arm. "You'll make a fine sheriff some day, Thomas, or even a federal marshal. I'm glad you want to stay."

Both Shaye and Thomas looked at James.

"Well, don't look at me," the younger man said. "I ain't goin' nowhere. Maybe I don't wanna be a sheriff someday, but right now I'm happy to be your deputy, Pa."

"I appreciate that, James," Shaye said, touching his youngest son's arm as well. One thing Mary had tried to instill in Shaye early on was that they ought to treat all three boys the same way and not show favorites.

"What do you want to do, James?" Thomas asked. "Be a banker, maybe?"

"Thomas . . ." James said warningly.

"A banker?" Shaye asked, smiling. "Is there something I should know?"

"Well . . ." Thomas said.

"Thomas!"

3

It was dusk when Ben Cardwell and Sean Davis rode into Vengeance Creek. Cardwell was shorter and stockier, but both men were in their thirties, wearing trail-worn clothes and well-used guns. The streets were just about empty, which suited them just fine.

"What do we know about this town?" Davis asked.

"Easy pickin's," Cardwell said.

"What about the law?"

"Name's Shaye, Dan Shaye," Cardwell said.

"Do we know him?"

"Supposed to be some hotshot lawman from Texas."

"So what makes this place so easy if he's a hot-shot lawman from Texas?"

"Don't worry," Cardwell said. "Even if we run into him, we'll have enough men backing us up."

"You keep tellin' me about these other men," Davis said. "How many? Are they any good?"

"They have guns and they'll know how to use them," Cardwell said.

"But are they any good?"

"It don't matter," Cardwell said. "We just have to put them between the law and us."

"Are they in for full shares?"

"There's only gonna be two full shares, Sean," Cardwell said, "and they're ours."

The Shayes had worked out a system they thought worked well—especially for Dan. Thomas was an early riser, so he opened the office in the morning. Dan came along later in the morning, and James in the afternoon. It was James who was in the office late, and who made late rounds. Sometimes Dan changed his schedule—he'd either show up early to help Thomas out or stay late to help James.

As they left the Carver House, Shaye announced he'd be staying late with James.

"Checkin' up on little brother, huh?" Thomas asked. "That's good, he needs some lookin' after."

They all knew that wasn't the reason, though. Shaye didn't want to go home to the house they shared just on the outskirts north of town. Alone with his thoughts, he'd just start thinking about his dead wife. Once that started, it would lead him to thinking about his deceased son. No, tonight he preferred to stay at work.

Thomas wasn't particularly anxious to go home alone either, but he kept that information to himself. He separated from his brother and father, saying he'd see them later at home. As soon as they were out of sight, he removed his badge and headed for the side of town that was across the dead line.

Cardwell and Davis were walking from the livery to the nearest hotel when they saw three men come out of the Carver House Café. There was still enough light for them to see the badges on the men's chests.

"Wait a minute," Cardwell said. "In here." He pushed Davis into a doorway.

"What are you doin'?"

"I just want to watch the local law for a minute."

They watched as the three men talked, then parted ways, one going off in one direction, the remaining two another way.

"Whataya think?" Davis asked.

"The sheriff's got some years on 'im," Cardwell said, "and one of the deputies looks like a green kid. It doesn't look like they'll be much trouble."

"What about the third one?"

"He looks capable enough," Cardwell said, stepping out of the doorway, "but one man's not gonna be a problem either. Come on, let's get that hotel room. In the morning we can take a look at the town."

4

Shaye and James made late rounds together in an awkward silence. They stopped in several saloons, checked the locked doors of some businesses, made sure the parts of the town that were shutting down for the night were secure, then headed back to the office.

"Pa?" James said on the way.

"Yes, James?"

"You miss Ma, don't you?"

Shaye hesitated, then said, "I miss Ma and Matthew, James."

"So do I."

After a couple more blocks Shaye said, "Why did you ask me that?"

"Um, you hide it real well," James said. "I mean, you're . . . quiet. Somebody lookin' at you couldn't tell, you know?"

"Men wear their grief differently, James," Shaye said. "Look at Thomas. He wears it as quietly as I do."

"But Thomas talk to me about it."

"He does?"

"Well . . . when I ask 'im."

Shaye put his arm around his younger son's shoulders. "James, whenever you ask me, I'll talk to you about it too. How's that?"

"That'd be good, Pa," James said. "That'd be real good."

When Cardwell and Davis registered at the Palace Hotel, Cardwell checked the register to see if any of his other men had arrived yet. They took one room with two beds, went upstairs to drop off their rifles and saddlebags.

"I saw you checkin' the book," Davis said. "Anybody else here yet?"

"No," Cardwell said, "we're first."

"I know any of these other fellas?"

"No," Cardwell said. "I figured you might have a problem double-crossing somebody you know."

"Not if there's enough money involved."

"This bank's supposed to hold a lot," Cardwell said. "Lots of ranchers in the area bank here."

"How do you know that?"

"I got somebody on the inside who's been keepin' me informed," Cardwell said.

"You trust them?"

"I trust the information."

"You gonna cut them in?"

"I'll have to see about that."

Davis went to the window and looked down at

the street. "Awful quiet around here once the sun goes down," he commented.

"We'll see how busy she is when the sun comes up," Cardwell said. "Gotta remember this is a weekday too. Folks worked all day and went home to eat and sleep. Weekend might be a little livelier."

"Why don't we find a part of town that's livelier now?" Davis asked. "I could sure use a beer and a woman about now."

"So could I," Cardwell said. "Let's go find 'em."

Thomas stopped in at the Road House Saloon, where the bartenders and saloon girls all knew him.

"Beer, Tom?" Al Baker asked him.

"Yep."

Baker, who not only worked the bar but owned the place, placed a cold mug in front of Thomas, who paid him. Thomas had long ago told Baker that whether he was wearing a badge or not, he paid his way. The older man respected him for that.

"Hi, Tommy." A blonde in a red dress sidled up to him, pressing her hips firmly against his. He could feel the warmth through both their clothes.

"Hello, Belinda."

"Been a while since you came to see me."

He didn't want to tell her that he only came around when he was depressed, and that he'd had a few good weeks until now.

"Been busy."

"Too busy for me?" She stuck out her lower lip and blinked her eyes. She was a few years older than him, and while he liked her, the little girl trick didn't suit her.

"Don't do that," he said. "You look silly when you do that."

"Ooh," she said, removing her hips from his, "somebody's in a bad mood."

"Foul," he corrected her. "I'm in a foul mood."

"Well," she said, "I'll leave you alone, then," and she flounced away.

Belinda was pretty enough, but not tonight. Tonight it would take a lot to change his mood— maybe even a miracle.

5

Thomas had kept his mood from James all day. Since he was the older brother, he believed he had to be strong for the younger. He knew that with Matthew gone, James needed him even more. But it was hard, being strong for somebody else. Sometimes you just needed to get away and give in to your mood.

He also didn't want his father knowing how he felt. Dan Shaye had enough on his mind. He'd lost a wife and a son. Thomas recognized that the deaths in their family had been hardest of all on his father. So when he felt down—or foul, as he felt right now—he came to this side of town, usually to this saloon, and drank alone.

And, as long as people left him alone, there was never any trouble.

Cardwell wanted a saloon with a lot of activity. He and Davis kept walking until they reached a more lively part of town. With several saloons to choose from, he picked the Road House. It was the biggest, the brightest, and the loudest.

"Now, this is my kind of place," Davis said, looking around. "Look at all the women."

"Don't get into trouble, Sean."

"How would I do that?" Davis asked innocently.

"By treating every woman you meet like a whore."

"Ain't they?"

"No," Cardwell said, "they're not. If you want a whore, then go find a whorehouse."

"Later," Davis said. "I want to try this place out first."

"There's a table," Cardwell said. "I'll grab it, and you go to the bar and get two beers."

"Okay."

Davis went to the bar, which didn't have much in the way of elbow room. He decided to force his way in, and by doing so, spilled some of Thomas's beer.

"Hey!" Thomas yelled. "Take it easy."

"I need two beers!" Davis shouted at the bartender, ignoring Thomas.

"There's room for everyone, you know," Thomas said. "No need to push."

Davis looked at Thomas and said, "Stay out of my way and you won't get pushed."

"Look, friend," Thomas said, "I'm just tryin' to give you some advice—"

"Keep your damned advice to yourself," Davis said.

"Hey, mister," the bartender, Al Baker, started, "you don't want to be talking to him that way, he's—"

"This man owes me a beer, Al," Thomas said. "Draw three and he'll pay for them."

Davis turned to face Thomas. Some of the other men at the bar sensed the trouble and backed off, giving the two men room.

"I'm only payin' for two beers," Davis said belligerently. "You pay for your own."

"I did pay for my own," Thomas said. "And you spilled it. That means you owe me one."

"I don't owe you shit!"

Baker set three mugs of beer on the bar and looked at the two men, wondering who was going to pay for what.

"Look," Thomas said, "I tried to do this nicely, so now I'm tellin' you—pay for the three beers."

Davis looked Thomas up and down. He saw a big man in his mid-twenties, at least ten years younger than him. He wasn't about to let some young punk tell him what to do.

"You know how to use that hogleg?" he asked, nodding at Thomas's revolve.

"I've been known to."

"Is it worth usin' it for a beer?"

Thomas spread his feet and planted them firmly beneath him. "It'll be worth it to teach you a lesson," he said, "and it might ease my bad mood."

"I'll take care of your mood—" Davis said, taking a step back. Before he could do anything else, though, Ben Cardwell stepped between the two men and planted his right hand against Davis's chest.

"Back off, Sean," he said with authority. "You did spill the man's beer. I saw you." He looked at Thomas. "My friend is clumsy. I apologize." Then he turned to the bar and tossed some coins on it. "That cover the three beers?"

"It covers it," Al Baker said.

"Enjoy your beer," Cardwell said to Thomas.

"What the hell—" Davis began.

"Let's sit down!" Cardwell snapped at him. "Now!"

He grabbed Davis by the arm and literally dragged him across the floor to their table.

"I thought he was gonna draw his gun for sure," Baker said to Thomas.

"He was," Thomas said. "He would have, if his friend hadn't stopped him."

"Then you would have killed him."

Thomas looked at Baker, picked up his beer and said, "Yes."

"Over a beer?"

Thomas put his elbows on the bar. "It would have been more than that."

"What the hell did you do that for?" Davis asked after Cardwell had forced him into a chair.

A large, ham-handed man, he easily pushed the slighter, shorter man into his seat.

"You didn't recognize that man?"

Davis looked across the room at Thomas, who had his back to him now. "No, should I?"

"We saw him earlier," Cardwell said. "He was wearing a badge."

"One of the deputies?"

"That's right. We don't need you gettin' into trouble with the law tonight, Sean."

Davis looked across the room again, but some of the men who had spread out to give them room to resolve their conflict before had closed ranks again, and he couldn't see the lawman.

"But . . . he wasn't wearin' his badge." The long, slender nose that gave his face the look of a weasel twitched.

"I noticed that."

"You sure—"

"I'm sure," Cardwell said.

Davis drank down a quarter of his beer.

"I would have killed him, you know."

"Probably," Cardwell said, "but that would have caused us a lot of trouble we don't need right now. So drink your beer and get used to the fact that you're not killin' anybody . . . not tonight, anyway."

6

"I thought I told you never to tell anyone I'm a deputy, Al," Thomas said to Baker.

"Thomas," Baker said, "everybody else in here knows it already. It was just those strangers—"

"I don't care," Thomas said. "If I wanted people to know—strangers—I'd wear the damned badge."

"Okay," Baker said, "sorry."

Thomas pushed his empty mug forward.

"Another?"

"Yeah."

"You usually nurse one," Baker said, picking up the mug. "This'll make two."

"Three," Thomas said, "counting the one that was spilled. Besides, what are you, my father?"

"Thomas—"

"I already have a father," he said. "Give me another beer."

"Comin' up."

Thomas made a point of not turning around to

look at the two strangers. No sense inviting another confrontation. Somebody might not walk away next time.

"I'm going home," Dan Shaye said. "You comin'?"

"I think I'm gonna walk around town some more, Pa," James said. "Make sure everything's all right."

They had just done that, so Shaye suspected James had something else on his mind. Maybe that gal Thomas had been talking about.

"Suit yourself, James," he said. "Just don't get yourself into trouble."

"I'll be careful, Pa."

"Good night, then."

Shaye walked home to a quiet house. He knew instinctively that Thomas was out, and not inside, asleep. Maybe that was where James was going, to find his brother.

Thomas finished that next beer and pushed the mug away. He was surprised at his own anger. He suspected it had been burning in his belly for a year, and two beers plus the better part of a third had probably fanned the flame. He felt ashamed when he realized who he was angry at.

He was considering another beer, wondering if it would put out the flame or fan it into an uncontrollable blaze when he felt someone sidle up next to him.

"James."

"Big brother."

"Want a beer?"

"How many have you had?"

"Enough."

"I'll skip it."

Thomas turned his head to look at his brother. "How'd you know where I was?"

"I looked."

"Why?"

"Something's been botherin' you, Thomas," James said. "I thought you might wanna talk about it."

"James—" Thomas started, but he stopped abruptly.

"Thomas?"

"Let's get out of here, James," Thomas said, "and I'll talk to you."

They turned away from the bar and headed for the door together under the watchful eyes of Ben Cardwell and Sean Davis.

"Why don't we follow them?" Davis asked. "We can get rid of them tonight."

"Yeah," Cardwell said, "that's all we need is two dead deputies showin' up in the mornin'— and the rest of our men aren't here yet."

"With the two deputies dead, you and me can do the job alone," Davis said.

"Sean," Cardwell said, "who makes all the plans?"

"Well . . . you, usually."

"And how do things turn out?"

"Well, okay, usually."

"Then shut up," Cardwell said, "and stop tryin' to do the thinkin'. You ain't cut out for it."

Thomas and James walked back toward the center of town, where it was quiet.

"What's goin' on, Thomas?" James asked.

Thomas didn't answer right away.

"Come on, Thomas," James said. "I know you're the older brother, and you're always there for me, but sometime you gotta let me be there for you . . . you know?"

Thomas looked at his little brother and realized he was right. If he was always going to be there for James, who would ever be there for him? His father? He couldn't very well do that, could he? After all, wasn't that who he was mad at?

"Tell me something, little brother," Thomas said. "Do you ever get angry?"

"What?" James asked. "Well, sure, yeah, I get mad sometimes."

"At who?"

James shrugged. "I get mad at Ethan Langer, for killin' Ma and Matthew."

"But he's dead," Thomas said. "You can't stay mad at a dead man."

"What are you sayin', Thomas?" James asked. "Who do you get mad at?"

Thomas hesitated. How would his brother react when he told him?

"I—I'm mad at Pa."

"At Pa?" James asked, surprised. "But . . . why?"

"I guess . . . deep down I blame him for Ma's death, and for Matthew's."

James stopped and grabbed Thomas's arm. "What are you talkin' about?" he asked. "Pa feels more pain about Ma's death than any of us—and Matthew. How could you blame him . . . that's just not fair."

"Well . . . I don't feel it all the time," Thomas said. "Sometimes it just . . . comes over me."

"Have you ever talked to Pa about it?"

"No," Thomas said, "I would never tell Pa that."

"Why not?"

"It would hurt him."

"If you're so mad at him, why don't you want to hurt him?" James asked.

"Because I love him."

James shook his head. "I'm confused."

"Imagine how I feel," Thomas said. "Look, James, this is just something I feel sometimes, okay? There's no need to tell Pa about it. Agreed?"

"Thomas—"

"If he ever needs to be told," Thomas said, "or if I ever need to tell him, I will. But it should be me who tells him, shouldn't it?"

James hesitated, then sighed and said, "Yes, I suppose it should."

"Okay, then," Thomas said, putting his hand on his brother's shoulder. "Then let's go home and go to bed."

James nodded and the two brothers began to walk again, this time toward the house they shared with their father.

Dan Shaye was usually the first to rise in the morning. It used to be his wife, Mary, who woke first and had breakfast on the table for her husband and her sons. Since her death—and since their move—he was unable to sleep for more than a few hours each night, so he got into the habit of rising first and trying to have breakfast ready for Thomas and James. The only problem was he was not a very good cook. On the trail he was passable—beans and coffee being his specialty—but in the kitchen he was a disaster. The boys often fretted about whether he would have breakfast ready when they woke up.

Today he made coffee, and nothing else. Took pity on his own stomach as well as his sons'.

"I thought we'd go to the café for breakfast today," he told them when they came into the kitchen.

"Suits me," Thomas said, frowning into his coffee. "Not that I'm insultin' your cookin' or nothin', Pa."

"That's all right, son," Shaye said. "I can insult my own cookin' enough for the three of us."

"Flapjacks ain't bad when you make 'em, Pa," James offered.

"I know," Shaye said, "I noticed how much butter and sugar syrup you slather on them because they're so good."

James looked away, put his coffee down half finished.

"All right, then, deputies," Shaye said. "I can see you're not even gonna finish the coffee this mornin', so let's go and get us somethin' decent to eat."

The café they usually ate breakfast in was a popular one in town. Off the main street, people still sought it out in the mornings, and town folk rarely recommended it to strangers.

"Your table's empty, Sheriff," the waiter said as they entered.

Shaye had always considered having a table waiting in the better restaurants a small thing to expect as part of the sheriff's job. Never one to demand any kind of graft from local businesses, this was the closest he ever came to a payoff.

James led the way, following the waiter to the table, and Thomas took the opportunity to tug on his father's arm and say, "There she is."

"There who is?" Shaye asked, looking around.

"Over against the wall, sittin' with an older woman," Thomas said. "That's the teller gal James is sweet on."

Shaye looked at the girl in question and saw a slender, pretty blonde about eighteen or nineteen.

"You don't know who that is?" he asked Thomas.

"A teller at the bank," Thomas said. "That's all I know."

"That's the mayor's daughter," Shaye said, "sittin' with the mayor's wife."

"Well, I'll be damned," Thomas said. "I guess I ain't never paid much attention to the mayor's family."

They hurried to catch up and sit with James, who had been careful to take a seat where he could look across the room at the mayor's daughter—although even he was not aware of her true identity.

Shaye wondered what the mayor would think if he knew that James was sweet on his daughter.

All three of them ordered steak and eggs, and Thomas added a stack of flapjacks. Shaye remembered having breakfast with all three of his sons and seeing Matthew pack away more food than the three of them put together. Recently he'd wondered if Thomas was trying to eat for Matthew as well. He noticed that his older son had put on some weight during the past year, but he was solid rather than fat. At six-two, he was four or five inches shorter than Matthew had been, and probably fifty pounds lighter.

Shaye was never able to stop thinking about his wife and his middle son, but he usually tried to push the memory somewhere, to the back of his mind, so it wouldn't interfere with his everyday life. At best, the grief made him numb, and at its worst it was unbearable. He tried not to let it show when he was with Thomas and James, and he knew it was the same with them.

"What were you two whisperin' about?" James asked when they had their food.

"Nothin'," Thomas said. He finished his first excellent cup of coffee quickly and poured a second one.

"Musta been somethin'," James said, eyeing his brother suspiciously. He looked longingly across the room at the mayor's daughter, then back at his brother, narrowing his eyes.

"Okay, so I tol' Pa about your teller gal."

"Thomas—"

"James," Shaye said, "that's the mayor's daughter."

"What?"

"I think her name is—"

"Nancy," James said. "Her name's Nancy. You sure she's the mayor's daughter?"

"I'm sure," Shaye said. "He must've got her the job in the bank."

"She's a right good teller, Pa," James said. "I

don't think she would have needed her pa to get her the job."

"Maybe not," Shaye said, stuffing some steak and eggs into his mouth.

"Better think twice about this one, little brother," Thomas said with a grin.

James frowned across the table at his brother. "You sayin' I ain't good enough for her?"

"I'm not sayin' that at all," Thomas said, "but considerin' this is the mayor we're talkin' about, somebody might say it."

"Thomas, what the—"

"That's enough, boys," Shaye said. "James, your brother just wants you to be careful. You know the kind of man the mayor is."

"But, Pa, you're the sheriff—"

"Mayor Timmerman just sees us as employees of the town, James," Shaye said, "and that's what we are. He don't see us as bein' on his level."

"He ain't so much," James muttered.

"Well, I agree with you there, son," Shaye said. "And I ain't tellin' you not to follow your heart. I'm just sayin' be ready for her to maybe have the same outlook her father does."

"She ain't like that," James said. "She's nice, Pa . . . she's right nice."

"I'm glad to hear it, James," Shaye said, "because you deserve a right nice girl . . . don't he, Thomas?"

"Huh?" Thomas looked up from his flapjacks. "Oh, yeah, right, Pa. He sure does."

After breakfast the three of them started walking toward the office together. Thomas happened to look across the street just as Ben Cardwell came out of the hotel.

"I'll see you at the office," he said to his father and brother.

Shaye looked across the street to see what had caught Thomas's attention. "What is it?" he asked.

"Just a stranger I met last night," Thomas said. "No big deal. I just want to talk to him."

"I'll come with you—" James started, but Thomas cut him off.

"That's okay, James," he said. "It's just one man. We're just gonna talk."

"Okay, Thomas," Shaye said. "Just watch yourself."

"Always, Pa."

Thomas started across the street as Shaye and James continued on to the sheriff's office.

* * *

Cardwell left Sean Davis snoring in the room and went downstairs for breakfast. He decided to walk around town to look for a place to eat rather than settling for the hotel dining room. As soon as he stepped outside, he saw the sheriff and the two deputies across the street. After a few moments, the deputy from the night before stepped into the street and started across. Cardwell thought that he and this deputy were probably destined to clash. He decided to wait where he was and let the man come to him. As the lawman got closer Cardwell could see that he was wearing his badge today.

Thomas knew the man was letting him come closer, and that suited him. He wondered where the other one was, and opened the conversation by asking.

"He's still asleep," Cardwell said. "When we're off the trail and in a real bed, he's a late riser."

"And what would be the late riser's name?"

"Davis, Sean Davis," Cardwell said. "You won't find his name on any posters."

"What about yours?"

"Ben Cardwell," the man said. "No paper on me either. We're just a couple of law abiding citizens."

"You law abidin' citizens figure on stayin' around town a little longer?" Thomas asked.

"We're not sure," Cardwell said.

"Headin' someplace?"

"We're not sure."

"What are you sure of?"

"Not much," Cardwell said. "That's how we like it. We just take it a day at a time."

"Well," Thomas said, "just keep a tight rein on your friend and there shouldn't be any trouble."

"I'm all for no trouble, Deputy," Cardwell said, "but you should know that we're always ready to . . . defend ourselves."

"Shouldn't be anything in town for you to defend yourselves against," Thomas said.

"Then it sounds like we won't have any trouble at all."

"Keep that in mind, then."

Thomas turned to leave, and Cardwell asked, "You got a name?"

"Shaye," Thomas said. "Thomas Shaye."

Cardwell frowned. "Ain't the sheriff's name Shaye?"

"He's my father," Thomas said. "You heard of him?"

"I might have heard somethin'."

"Maybe you heard he's got less patience that I have."

"Naw . . . that wasn't it. What about the other deputy? The young one?"

"My brother."

"You fellas keep it all in the family, huh?"

"That's right," Thomas said. "We're closer than most lawmen, and we really watch each other's backs."

"Nobody watchin' your back now, are they?"

Thomas looked Cardwell in the eye and said, "I don't need anybody watchin' my back now, do I?"

"I guess not," Cardwell said, raising his hands to shoulder level and spreading them. He even wiggled his fingers. "There's no danger here, Deputy."

"I hope it stays that way."

A block away Dan and James Shaye had stopped. They were watching Thomas and the other man talk in front of the hotel.

"Somethin' happened last night at the saloon," James said, "but I don't know what."

"Which saloon?"

"The Road House."

Shaye did not take his eyes from the two men a block away, but he wanted to look at James.

"What was Thomas doin' at that end of town?"

"I don't know, Pa."

"Okay," Shaye said, "that part doesn't really matter now."

"What part does, Pa?"

"I want to find out what happened last night," Shaye said. "I'll go and talk to Al Baker, he owns the Road House—"

"I can do that, Pa," James said.

Thomas turned to walk away from the other man, then turned back.

"All right, James," Shaye said. "Go and do that." Shaye told his son where Baker lived. "He stays open late, so he'll be asleep now."

"I'll wake him up."

"You do that."

James didn't move.

"Do it now, James."

"Yes, Pa."

9

Shaye got back to the sheriff's office well before Thomas. He knew he could ask his son what had happened at the Road House Saloon the night before, but if Thomas was going to places like that and not telling anyone, there had to be a reason. He'd leave it to James to find out what that reason was.

Thomas entered the office and walked right to the stove to put on a pot of coffee, which they kept going all day.

"How did it go?"

Thomas turned and looked at his father. "You ought to know," he said. "You watched the whole time."

"Just watching your back, Thomas," Shaye said. "It doesn't mean I don't trust you, it just means that I like to keep my deputies alive."

"If it was a deputy who wasn't your son, would you feel the same?" Thomas asked.

"Exactly the same."

"Then fine," the younger man said. "Then we don't have a problem, do we?"

"I never thought we did," Shaye said. "So what did you find out about the stranger?"

"Strangers," Thomas said. "There's two of them, and they're just . . . drifting, or so this one says."

"You get their names?"

"Yes." He gave the names to his father, who reached for his stack of wanted flyers. "Cardwell said there was no paper on either of them."

"He's probably right," Shaye said, "if he gave you their real names."

"Well, if he gave me phony names, then we can only go by the likeness of the posters," Thomas said. "That means I should look through them."

"Be my guest."

Thomas sat opposite his father and pulled the stack of flyers into his lap. "Where's James?"

"He said he had to run an errand."

Thomas smirked. "At the bank, I'll bet."

"You're probably right."

While going through the flyers Thomas asked, "You gonna talk to the mayor?"

"About what?"

"About his daughter and James."

"Thomas," Shaye said, "has James even talked to the girl beyond bank business?"

"Not that I know of."

"Then I don't think there's a relationship there worth talkin' to the mayor about, do you?"

"No, sir," Thomas said, "I guess you're right."

The water on the stove began to boil, so Shaye went over to drop the coffee in while Thomas continued to go through the flyers.

James knew that Al Baker lived right above the Road House. There was a stairway on the side of the building leading up to a door, which James first knocked on, then pounded on.

"All right, all right!" an annoyed voice came from inside. "I'm comin'!"

The door swung open and Al Baker squinted out at James from beneath heavy, puffy eyelids.

"What the hell—"

"Deputy Shaye, Mr. Baker," James said. "That's James Shaye."

"Whataya want?"

"Just a few questions about last night," James said. "Can I come in?"

"Nothin' happened last night," Baker said. "I never even called for the law."

"Somethin' happened between my brother and two men," James said. "I want to know what that was."

"Why don't you ask your brother?"

"Because I'm askin' you."

Baker scowled and said, "Okay, come on in."

He backed away from the door to let James enter. Baker lived in one large room, and in the corner was a bed with a naked blond woman asleep.

She was lying with her back to the men, and James caught himself admiring her shapely backside before he caught himself and looked away.

"I won't keep you long," he said to Baker, trying to hide the fact that he was flustered.

"That's just one of the girls," Baker said, scratching his head. He was wearing a pair of soiled long johns, and the room itself matched him. James wondered if the man ever cleaned it, but from the smell, he doubted it. He didn't know how any woman could stand it. "Does she bother you? I can cover her up."

"I just want you to tell me what happened last night."

Briefly, Baker told James about Thomas's run-in with one man, and how the other man had stepped in to defuse the situation.

"I tried to tell them your brother was a deputy, but he stopped me," Baker said.

"He wasn't wearin' his badge?"

"No," Baker said, "he never wears it when he comes in."

James tried to remember if his brother was wearing his badge when he saw him, but couldn't.

"Al . . ." the woman called plaintively from the bed.

James looked over as the woman rolled onto her back, revealing her large breasts. She reached down between her thighs and started to scratch herself.

"I'm comin', sweetie," Baker said. "Are we done, Deputy?"

James averted his eyes once again, but could hear the woman's nails on her skin. He started for the door.

"What did the two men do after Thomas and I were gone?" he asked Baker, standing outside with the door open.

"They just had a few more beers and then left," Baker said with a shrug. "See? Nothin' really happened."

"Okay, Mr. Baker," James said, then thought of one more question. "How many times a week does my brother come into your place, without his badge?"

Baker shrugged and said, "A couple, sometimes three. Not more than that."

"Had there ever been trouble before?"

"No," Baker said. "Mostly he nurses one beer and then leaves."

"Okay, thanks."

From inside they both heard the woman called, "Alllllll!"

"Gotta go," Baker said, and closed the door.

James hurried down the stairs because he didn't want to hear what was going on in that room.

10

Thomas was out doing morning rounds when James returned to the office.

"What did you find out?" Shaye asked.

James took a moment to pour a cup of coffee, then relayed everything he'd learned to his father while seated with his feet up on the desk.

"Doesn't sound like much," Shaye said.

"I guess not," James said. "Coulda been more, though, if that other man hadn't stepped in."

"Cardwell and Davis," his father said. "We don't know if that's their real names."

"What about posters?"

"Thomas checked," Shaye said. "He didn't recognize their likeness on any of them."

"So what do we do?"

"Nothing," Shaye said. "They haven't broken any laws here. Let's just keep an eye on them."

"Me?"

"Yes," Shaye said, "you."

"What about Thomas?"

"I'll talk to Thomas," Shaye said. "Maybe we should just all stay on the job at the same time while they're in town."

"Okay with me."

"Then get your boots off my desk and get out there."

James dropped his feet to the floor and said, "Yes, sir."

Ben Cardwell kicked the bed and shouted at his partner, "Time to get up, goddamn it!"

Davis leaped into a sitting position, staring around him wildly. He went for his gun, but Cardwell had wisely removed it from the holster hanging on the bed post.

"Lookin' for this?" he asked, holding the gun out. "I coulda put a bullet in you while you slept. Might as well have, you sleep like the dead, anyway."

Davis looked around, then asked, "We bring any whores back here with us last night?"

"Not a one."

"Damn!"

He rubbed his hands over his face, and suddenly his eyes focused and he was awake.

"Whatsamatter?" he asked.

Cardwell tossed his gun onto the bed and said, "Time to get up, is all."

"Breakfast?"

"I had breakfast," Cardwell said. "More like lunch, for you."

"You been out, already?" Davis swung his feet to the floor, let his hands hang between his knees for a moment. He was wearing off-white long johns which at one time had been white. His legs were long and skinny, his knees knobby.

"Out and back," Cardwell said. "Had me a conversation with the law."

"The sheriff?" Davis looked surprised.

"The deputy," Cardwell said.

"The one from last night?"

"Yeah."

"What did that bastard want?"

"Just some questions about what we're doin' in town."

"What did you tell him?"

"Not much," Cardwell said, "but they're probably gonna be watchin' us."

"So are we callin' off the job?"

"No," Cardwell said, "we're goin' ahead with the job. In fact, them watchin' us is probably gonna help us with the job."

"Howzat gonna help?" Davis asked.

"Get yourself dressed and meet me downstairs," Cardwell said, heading for the door, "and I'll tell you."

11

Cardwell and Davis spent the day sitting out in front of the hotel. James spent the day across the street watching them. Other strangers rode into town, but James didn't pay them any mind. His job was to keep an eye on these two men. The fact that they hardly moved all afternoon was boring to him, but hardly significant.

Later in the afternoon, Thomas came to join him.

James was sitting in a wooden chair outside the general store. Thomas perched his hip on a nearby barrel and looked across the street.

"What have they been doin'?" he asked.

"Nothin'," his brother said. "Just sittin' there, all afternoon."

"That's it?"

James shrugged.

"Anybody talk to them?"

"Thomas," James said, shaking his head, "they hardly have said a word to each other."

"Well," Thomas said, "why don't you take a break and I'll watch for a while."

"You won't get any argument from me," James said, standing up. "I haven't eaten anything since breakfast."

Thomas took his brother's place in the chair. "Take a couple of hours, James," he said.

Before he left, James said, "You might want to think about something I've been wondering about for a while."

"Like what?"

"If they strand up and go separate ways," James asked, "which one will you follow?"

"You're right," Thomas said. "I'll have to give that some thought."

As James walked away, Thomas looked at the two men across the street and instinctively knew which one he would follow.

"They changed deputies," Davis said.

"I can see that."

"So . . . what are we gonna do?"

"Have you been keeping count?" Cardwell asked.

"Of what?"

Cardwell closed his eyes. "Okay, how many of our men have ridden in since we've been sittin' here?"

"Uh . . . a few?"

"Six," Cardwell said. "Six of our men are here."

"Six . . . well, hey, that's all of them."

"Right," Cardwell said, glad that at least Davis knew that much. "So we're all in place."

"Except us," Davis said.

"Oh, don't worry," Cardwell said, "when the time comes we'll be in position."

The other six men had strict instructions from Cardwell not to be seen together in more than twos. They also had instructions to ignore both Cardwell and Davis whenever they saw them. And their final direction from Cardwell was when to be at the bank, because that's what they were all in town to do—rob the bank.

But Cardwell had the robbery mapped out in steps, and each of the men had his own steps to take. In the event the job was called off, Cardwell would make direct contact with the others or would have Davis do it.

But so far Ben Cardwell had not seen anything in town that would make him change his plans. The sheriff might have been impressive when he was younger, but not now, and the fact that his deputies were his two sons—well, that didn't exactly inspire Cardwell to cancel his plans either.

Things were going to go off as planned.

12

Shaye was sitting in his office while his sons took turns keeping an eye on the strangers. When the door opened and a man entered, he looked up, expecting one of the boys. Instead it was Harry Chalmers, who was a clerk for the mayor and, like him, also a lawyer. Chalmers was about the same age as Thomas.

"Sheriff."

"Afternoon, Harry. What can I do for you?"

"Mayor Timmerman sent me over to tell you—uh, ask you—to come over and see him."

"What's botherin' the mayor?"

"I don't know, sir," Chalmers said. "He doesn't tell me everything."

"That's funny," Shaye said, "I thought he did, Harry."

"Sheriff," Chalmers said, "I don't think the mayor tells anyone everything, not even Mrs. Timmerman."

"Uh-huh," Shaye said. "Okay, tell the mayor I'll be over shortly."

"Shortly?"

"Oh, you thought I'd come right over with you?"

"Well . . ."

"Go back and tell the mayor . . . shortly."

"Okay," Chalmers said, "but, uh, today, right?"

"Yes, Harry," Shaye said, "today."

Shaye didn't make the mayor wait very long, just long enough for the man to realize he wouldn't come running whenever he was called. About a half hour later he appeared in the mayor's office.

"Ah, Sheriff," Harry Chalmers said from behind his desk, "I'll tell the mayor you're here."

"You do that, Harry."

Chalmers knocked on the mayor's door and entered, then returned and held the door open.

"You can go right in, Sheriff."

"Thank you, Harry."

Shaye slid past the clerk into the mayor's office. Timmerman remained seated, making a statement that way. He was a large, barrel-chested man in his fifties who, even in just the year Shaye and his sons had been in town, had put on weight. Shaye knew they were the same age, but Timmerman looked considerably older.

"Ah, Sheriff Shaye," Timmerman said, "thanks so much for coming over."

"Harry seemed to think it was important,

Mayor," Shaye said. "Some town business I should know about?"

"No, Sheriff," Timmerman said, "it's more of a, uh, personal matter. Have a seat, will you?"

Shaye sat down opposite the man, wondering what kind of personal business they could possibly have.

"Sheriff . . . Daniel . . . can I call you Daniel?"

"I prefer Dan, if that's all right with you, Mayor."

"All right, Dan," Timmerman said.

Shaye knew the man's name was William, but he wasn't about to call him "William," or "Will" or "Bill," for that matter. "Mayor" was good enough for him.

"What's on your mind, Mayor?"

"Well, actually . . . Dan . . . I want to talk to you about one of your sons."

"One of my deputies?"

"I know they're your deputies, but I need to talk to you about one of them as your son."

"And which one would that be, Mayor?"

"The young one," Timmerman said, "James."

Shaye took a moment to study the mayor and scratch his head.

"What about James?" he finally asked.

"You know my daughter, Nancy."

"Not really," Shaye said. "I mean, I know you have a daughter, but I don't know her."

"Well, Nancy works at the bank," Timmerman said, "and it has come to my attention that your son James has been, uh, well . . . hanging around my daughter."

"Hanging around?" Shaye asked. "What does that mean, mayor?"

"Well, he's always around the bank, and this morning he was in the café where my wife and daughter were having breakfast."

"Mayor," Shaye said, "my son Thomas and I were both with James in the café this morning. We were all having breakfast there. Is that a problem?"

"Well . . . no, not as such, but—"

"What does that mean, 'as such'?" Shaye demanded.

"Sheriff," Timmerman said, "I'm sure you appreciate my position in the community."

"As a lawyer? Or as mayor?"

"Both, actually, as well as a father."

"We're both fathers."

"But that's where our similarities end," Timmerman said. "I'm a politician, Sheriff."

"And I'm a lawman," Shaye said. "Maybe that's why I'm havin' trouble understanding what you're trying to say here. You're talkin' like a politician." Shaye leaned forward. "Why don't you just say what you want to say right out?"

Timmerman sat back in his chair, as if trying to maintain his distance from Shaye.

"All right, then," he finally said. "I don't think it would be a good idea for your son, James, to pursue a relationship with my daughter."

"What makes you think James has any intention of doin' that?" Shaye asked.

"Nancy has told me how he comes around the bank and . . . looks at her."

"My son goes to the bank because he has a deposit there."

"So he's not interested in Nancy?'

"Not that I know of," Shaye said. "She's kind of a . . . skinny thing, ain't she?"

"Nancy's very pretty," Timmerman said. "Everyone in town knows that."

"Mayor, did Nancy tell you that James has spoken to her? Told her he's interested in her?"

"Well, no—"

Shaye stood up. "I don't think we have anything else to talk about," he said. "My son is not interested in your daughter."

Shaye walked to the door, opened it and stopped there. He looked at Timmerman, who was still leaning back in his chair.

"But just for the record," Shaye said, "don't ever try to tell me that my son is not good enough for your daughter."

"I wasn't—"

"That's exactly what you were tryin' to do," Shaye said, "in your politician way."

Shaye walked out without another word. He closed the door gently, although he wanted to slam it, then walked out past Chalmers and closed the outer door gently as well. Moments later Chalmers heard the downstairs door slam.

* * *

After James had some food and took care of some other business, he returned to spell Thomas.

"Any change?" he asked, taking the seat.

"Yeah," Thomas said. "They had a conversation."

13

Instead of going back to his office, Shaye walked around town for a while, waiting for his anger at the mayor to dissipate. He did not walk anywhere near the hotel where James and Thomas were keeping an eye on Cardwell and Davis. Instead, he walked in the other direction and eventually found himself in front of the Road House Saloon. He decided to go in and have a beer. The place was half full, and finding a spot at the bar was easy.

"Sheriff Shaye," Al Baker said. "You never come in here."

"I'm here now, Al," Shaye said. "I'll have a beer."

"Sure," Baker said, "comin' up."

He went to draw the beer, and the other men at the bar moved to give Shaye more room. They all knew the story of Shaye tracking down the Langer gang.

Baker returned with a beer and put it down in

front of Shaye. "I told your boy everythin' I knew about Thomas, Sheriff," the barkeep said.

"I'm not here about that, Al," Shaye said. "I'm just here to have a beer."

"Oh," Baker said, "well, okay. On the house?"

"I'll pay."

"Like father, like son."

Shaye put a coin on the bar and said, "What?"

"Thomas," Baker said, picking up the coin. "He always insists on payin' too."

"When did Thomas start comin' in here, Al?"

Baker thought a moment, then said, "Coupla months ago, I guess."

"He ever say why?"

"No, not exactly."

"What do you mean, not exactly?"

"I've seen a lot of men drink, Sheriff," Baker said. He leaned his elbows on the bar. "I can usually tell why, just from lookin' at them. I know when they're drinkin' to wash down the dust, I know when they're drinkin' because they need to, and I know when they're drinkin' out of anger."

"And Thomas?"

Baker straightened up. "He was a pretty angry young man."

Shaye drank half his beer down and thought that over.

"Sheriff?"

"Yeah, Al?"

"You're pretty angry right now, aren't you?"

Baker moved down the line to serve someone else.

Shaye could see that the bartender had obviously been telling the truth about his ability to read people, which meant he was right about Thomas as well. And if Thomas was angry, who else could he be possibly be angry at than his father?

Shaye finished his beer and left the saloon.

"Ain't we at least goin' to a saloon tonight?"

"No."

"But we been sittin' here all day, Ben," Davis complained.

"We went inside to eat in the dining room."

"Yeah, but other than that we been sittin' here all day with them watchin' us. I gotta go do somethin'."

Cardwell stood up. "I tell you what. I'm goin' to the room. You can do whatever you want to with the rest of the night."

"That suits me," Davis said, standing up quickly.

Cardwell grabbed his arm and pointed a finger at him. "Just don't get in no trouble, understand?"

"I understand."

Cardwell released the man's arm and stepped inside the hotel lobby. Immediately, he ducked to one side so he could look out the window. He watched as the deputy across the street—the young one—made up his mind whether to follow Davis or stay put.

*   *   *

James watched the two men stand up, have a brief conversation, and then split up. One went into the hotel and the other started walking down the street. He took just a moment to decide to follow the one who was on the move, as the other one appeared to be staying put.

Thomas was sitting at the desk in the office when Shaye walked in. "Well, where have you been?"

"I had a meetin' with the mayor."

"What about?"

"Your brother."

"What did James do?"

"Nothin'," Shaye said. "Get out of my chair."

Thomas gave up his father's chair, walked around the desk and sat down again. "What are you so mad about?" he asked.

"Goddamn Timmerman thinks your brother ain't good enough for his daughter."

"He said that?"

"Not in so many words," Shaye replied, "but that's what he meant."

"Pa, James ain't said two words to that gal except to make a deposit."

"I know that."

"So what makes the mayor think—"

"Apparently the girl has told her father that James is . . . watchin' her."

"Watchin'?" Thomas asked. "He peeks in the

window at her sometimes, but it ain't like he's followin' her or nothin'."

"I'll have a talk with him," Shaye said. "I don't need this aggravation. Not now."

Thomas knew what his father meant. He suspected they were all feeling the effects of this unwanted anniversary.

"Where is James?"

"Watchin' those two strangers," Thomas said. "Speakin' of which, I better get over there and spell him again."

"Once they turn in, forget about them, Thomas," Shaye said. "They're probably passin' through, just like they said."

"Okay, Pa. You want me to talk to James—"

"Don't mention anythin' to James," Shaye said, cutting him off. "I'll take care of it."

"Sure, Pa."

Shaye stared at the door after Thomas closed it behind him. He had sensed no anger in his oldest son, but he knew it was there. He knew this time would come, when they'd mark one year since the deaths of Mary and Matthew, but he'd had no idea how it would affect them all. He wondered if there was anger inside James as well.

14

Cardwell watched out the front window, waiting for the other deputy to come. When the man showed up, he looked around, obviously trying to decide his next move. If he came into the hotel to check on him . . . but he didn't. He hesitated a moment, then turned and walked back the way he had come.

Cardwell left the room, went downstairs and out the back door.

Of the six other strangers who had come to town, Cardwell wanted to find Simon Jacks. He knew that Jacks would seek out a back table at the smallest, quietest saloon and wait there for him to find him—which he did, at the third saloon he checked.

"What took you so long?" Jacks asked as Cardwell sat down across from him. "You saw me ride in."

"We saw all of you ride in," Cardwell said, "but Davis managed to attract some attention to us."

"What kind of attention?"

"The law kind."

"I told you a long time you should get rid of him."

"I will," Cardwell said, "after this job is over."

"He still thinks he's gettin' a full share?"

"Yes."

"All right," Jacks said, "you might as well get a beer and tell me everything that's happened."

Simon Jacks did not look anything like the hard case Ben Cardwell knew he was. His clothes were not flashy, and the gun he wore on his hip was well worn and unremarkable. You couldn't tell the kind of man he was unless you looked into his eyes.

Jacks was about ten years older than Cardwell, and had been working with him for five years. He was more experienced than Cardwell, but Simon Jacks had never had the desire to be anyone's leader. He was perfectly happy when someone gave him a job to do, and then paid him when it was done.

He listened intently while Cardwell explained everything that had happened since their arrival in town, after first getting himself a beer from the bar.

"I hope the rest of the men are smarter than Davis," Cardwell finished.

"Don't worry," Jacks said. "They won't attract

any unwanted attention. Tell me about these deputies."

"They're young," Cardwell said, "and brothers, and their father is the sheriff."

"A sheriff with sons as deputies?"

"Yeah, so?"

Jacks sat forward. "What's their name?"

"Shaye," Cardwell said. "Why?"

"The father, he's Dan Shaye?"

"Yeah. He was supposed to be some kind of big lawman in Texas a while back."

"Jesus," Jacks said, "this changes things, Ben."

"How?"

"You don't know who these men are?"

"Local law—"

"Do you know about the Langer gang?"

Cardwell hesitated, then said, "Wait a minute. They're the ones?"

Jacks nodded. "They hunted down the Langer gang, killed them all except for Ethan. Him they crippled and then put in Huntsville."

"Okay, wait," Cardwell said, "wait a minute. This can still work."

"You still want to go ahead with the job?"

"I've planned it too long to let it go now," Cardwell said. "We know who Shaye is, and his sons. We can deal with them."

Jacks sat back in his chair and stared at Cardwell.

"Well, you're the planner," he said finally. "What do you want to do?"

"We've got the deputies watchin' us," Cardwell said. "Chances are they've been so busy doin' that, they haven't even noticed you and the others."

"Nobody's checking into a hotel," Jacks said. "They'll bed down wherever they find room. I don't want their names showing up on hotel registers. Let 'em sleep in a boardinghouse, stable, I don't care."

"That's good."

"What about Shaye himself?" Jacks asked. "Is he watching like the others?"

"No," Cardwell said. "We haven't even talked to him. I've only spoken with the oldest son. I think his name is Thomas." He looked at Jacks. "Do you know Shaye?"

"No," the man said, "but I've heard of him."

"He's old," Cardwell said. "He got to be fifty. Can't be the man he used to be."

"Man enough to track down the entire Langer gang with only his two sons."

"Okay, okay," Cardwell said, "so we'll be careful. We're still gonna do this, Simon."

"Hey," Jacks said, "just point me in the direction you want me to go."

"What about the others?" Cardwell asked. "Will they recognize the lawman's name?"

"Maybe not," Jacks said, "but why do they have to hear it?"

"Good point."

"Get us another couple of beers," Jacks said, "and we'll drink to gettin' this done."

15

Thomas didn't like the fact that James was not in front of the hotel. The men must have moved after it got dark and he'd followed them—but to where?

After he left the hotel he kicked himself for not going inside and checking with the clerk. Maybe one or both of the men had gone to their room. And maybe his father was right, and they were just a couple of drifters. Maybe he'd overreacted at the Road House when one of them bumped him and spilled his beer. If he'd let it go, there would have been no confrontation.

But one of them—the one called Cardwell—he was too slick for Thomas's liking. There was something about him that said he was more than a drifter.

He stopped in the street, halfway between the hotel and the sheriff's office. Should he go back and check? Or should he keep looking for James? He hadn't passed his brother on the way, so apparently James hadn't gone back to the office.

There was only one other part of town they could have gone to.

James followed Sean Davis to the Road House Saloon but did not go in after him. Maybe the man had a one-track mind and was looking for Thomas. James got close enough to the window to look inside. He saw Davis standing at the bar, but his brother was nowhere in sight. He decided to stay right there by the window so he could watch the man's every move. Because he was so intent on this, he was startled when Thomas came up next to him.

"Jesus!" he said. "You scared the hell out of me!"

"Sorry," Thomas said. "When I found you were gone from the hotel, I got worried. Are they inside?"

"One of them is."

Thomas leaned to look in the window. "That's Davis. Where's the other one, Cardwell?"

"He went into the hotel. I had to decide whether to stay there or follow this one, and I needed to decide fast."

"Don't sound so defensive," Thomas said, putting his hand on his brother's shoulder. "You did the right thing."

"Thanks, Thomas."

"What's he been doin' in there?"

"Just drinkin'."

"Pa's probably right."

"About what?"

"He said they were probably just driftin' through," Thomas explained, "just like they said."

James looked at his brother, whose face was bathed in yellow light from inside the saloon.

"But you don't believe that."

"Somethin' just doesn't feel right to me."

"Should we go in?" James asked.

"No," Thomas said, "that would be askin' for trouble."

"What, then?"

Thomas straightened, moved away from the window. "Let's just forget it."

"What?"

"This whole thing got started because of me," Thomas said. "I say let it drop. Leave them alone. They'll probably leave town tomorrow, anyway."

"But—"

"And by spending so much time and attention on them, who knows what we've missed?"

"What about Pa?" James asked. "He's been around. Nothin' gets by him."

"In case you haven't noticed, Pa hasn't been himself lately," Thomas said.

"Neither have we, I think."

"You're right about that," Thomas said. "This . . . anniversary has been hard on all of us."

"The anniversary of Ma's death," James said. "Matthew didn't die till later—weeks later. What's gonna happen when that day's anniversary comes?"

"I don't know," Thomas said, laying his hand on his brother's shoulder. "I guess we'll just have to be better prepared for that day. Come on, we've had a long day of wasting time on these two."

Older brother tugged younger brother away from the saloon, with James casting dubious glances back. He wasn't sure about his brother's decision, but he allowed himself to be led away.

As Thomas led James away from the Road House, he wondered if he should tell him about their father's conversation with the mayor. But no, his pa wanted to do that himself. But not tonight. Thomas thought if he took James home now maybe he could get his brother to turn in before their father got home. He knew his father wouldn't wake James, but would wait until morning. And maybe, in the light of a new day, everything would look a little better.

Shaye sat as his desk, grateful that this day was coming to an end. He too was remembering when Matthew died, and that they still had the first anniversary of that day to live through. Once they were past that, then maybe they could get on with their lives. If the boys did both choose to go off on their own, then it would be up to him to decide their next move. Was Vengeance Creek just a stop along the way?

And if so, along the way to where?

16

When Cardwell looked out the window the next morning, he was surprised. Neither of the deputies were across the street.

"Wake up!" he shouted at Sean Davis, snoring in the next bed.

"Wha . . . ?" Davis came awake and grabbed for his gun, which was resting on the dresser across the way. Cardwell had learned long ago that the other man's first instinct upon waking was to go for his pistol.

"Wake up, Sean," Cardwell said. "Come on, we need to talk."

Davis looked at Cardwell and tried to focus his eyes. "Whatsamatta?" he asked.

"Were you followed to the saloon last night?" Cardwell asked.

Davis frowned. "I dunno."

"Damn it!" Cardwell walked across the room, picked up the pitcher of water that was on the dresser, and dumped the contents over Sean Davis's head.

"Hey— Wha—" Davis sputtered as he leaped from the bed. "What the hell are you doin'?"

"Tryin' to wake you up."

"Well, I'm awake!" Davis shouted. He ran his hands over his wet face, then looked down at himself.

"Then listen to me," Cardwell said. "And answer my questions. Did the deputy follow you last night?"

"I don't know."

"Well, think about it," Cardwell said. "I saw him leave after you, but did he follow you? Did he watch you all night? Did he trail you back here? Come on, man!"

"I dunno!" Davis said. "I drank a lot. I can't remember."

"Well, they're not outside today," Cardwell said, looking out the window again.

Davis finally started to wake up. He began stripping his wet long johns off.

"That's a good thing, right?"

Cardwell looked at him. "I adjusted my plan to include them. If they're not around, I'll have to adjust again."

"Go back to the original plan."

"It must be nice to have nothin' goin' on in your head," Cardwell said.

"Least I sleep soundly."

Cardwell was aware that he didn't sleep well, tended to toss and turn most of the night.

"Get yourself dressed," he said. "We have a busy day today."

Naked, Davis reached down and scratched his crotch. Cardwell averted his eyes, said, "I'll meet you downstairs," and left.

Cardwell went down to the lobby, hoping to see one of the deputies there. He was disappointed. Now he wasn't sure which plan to go with, which distressed him, but he was sure of one thing.

The Vengeance Creek bank was getting robbed today.

Shaye woke to the smell of bacon. When he got down to the kitchen, he found his youngest son making breakfast.

"James?"

"Eggs and bacon, Pa," James said. "I remember watchin' Ma make it."

Shaye also smelled something burning, and wrinkled his nose at it. He looked over at the oven, where smoke was apparently in the process of dissipating.

James saw where his father was looking and said, "I guess I didn't watch so carefully when it came to biscuits."

"What's that smell?" Thomas asked, coming into the room.

"Your brother made breakfast."

"Made it," Thomas asked, "or burned it?"

"Sit down, shut up, and eat," Shaye said, taking a seat at the table.

James served out three plates of scrambled eggs and bacon, and then placed a platter of burnt biscuits on the table. He finished by putting out three cups of coffee, then sitting down himself.

"You came in late last night, Pa," Thomas said.

"I was at the office."

"Workin'?"

Shaye shrugged. "Thinkin', mostly."

"About what, Pa?" James asked, which drew a look from his older brother.

"About us, mostly," Shaye said, not noticing the exchange. "What we're gonna do, where we're gonna go, that sort of thing."

"Not thinkin' about those two strangers?" James asked.

"Can't suspect every stranger who comes to town, James," Shaye said. "What'd they do last night, by the way?"

"One of them turned in early," Thomas said, "the other one went to the Road House Saloon. We left him there and came home."

"Just as well," Shaye said. "There have probably been some other strangers who came into town while you boys were occupied with them and I was . . . well, distracted."

"Maybe we should check into that today," Thomas said. "Me and James can check the hotels and rooming houses, maybe even stop in at the saloons."

"That sounds good," Shaye said. "Why don't you boys do that?"

"And what are you gonna do, Pa?" Thomas asked.

"Me?" Shaye asked. "I'm gonna work on gettin' my head on straight."

Cardwell and Davis stepped out of the hotel and looked around.

"Maybe they are watchin' us," Davis said, "only we can't see them."

Cardwell lifted his head, as if smelling the air. "No," he said. "I'd know if I was bein' watched."

"Then why did they stop?"

"Maybe we convinced them we're harmless."

Davis smiled. "Well, they're gonna learn that's wrong, ain't they, Ben?"

"A lot of people are gonna learn somethin' new today."

Thomas and James left the house before their father, stopping just outside to discuss their options.

"Let's split up," Thomas said. "We'll cover more ground."

"We can cover each other's backs if we stay together," James argued.

"Cover each other from what?" Thomas asked.

"You heard what Pa said. We can't suspect every stranger. All we got to do today is identify them."

"Okay," James said with a shrug. "You're the big brother."

"Hey," Thomas said, "we're equal as deputies, aren't we?"

"We are?" James asked, looking after his brother as Thomas walked off.

Simon Jacks had the luxury of getting himself a hotel room, while the other five men just had to find a place to lay their heads for the night—as long as it wasn't someplace where they had to write their names down, like a hotel. They could have used phony names, but Jacks didn't even want anyone to be able to count the bodies.

Jacks's hotel was a small, run-down building on a side street, because all he needed was a bed. When he came out and found Cardwell waiting for him, he was surprised.

"What the hell?" he said.

"They're gone," Cardwell said.

"Where?"

"Who knows?" Cardwell said. "All I know is they ain't watchin' us right now, so it's time to go."

"Where's Davis?"

"He'll be there. The others?"

"They'll be ready."

"Then let's go."

* * *

Nancy Timmerman entered the bank and exchanged good-mornings with the other employees.

"Nancy?"

She turned and saw the manager, Fred Baxter, standing in the doorway of his office.

"Yes, Mr. Baxter?"

"Would you come inside for a moment, please?"

He turned and went into the office, and Nancy shuddered. He wasn't as old as her father, but he was close, and she hated the way he looked at her. He'd given her the job because of her father, and so far all he'd done was look at her. Maybe today was the day he crossed the line, and she'd have to give up the job because of it—or ask her father to fire the man, since he owned the bank. So far she hadn't been brave enough to talk to her father about it, because he wanted her to learn the banking business. She thought that if she were a son—which her father always wanted and had never gotten—he probably would have installed her as assistant manager instead of as a lowly teller.

She steeled herself, then marched into the manager's office to see what he wanted.

Cardwell and Jacks approached the bank slowly, eyeing their men, who were scattered about the area of the bank.

"Where's Davis?" Jacks asked.

"He's bringin' the horses."

"Why'd you give him that job?" Jacks asked. "He didn't complain about that?"

"Originally I was gonna take him into the bank with us, but I decided not to. Since you and me are the only ones who are gonna get full shares, it might as well be just us."

Jacks checked his pocket watch. "Bank'll open in five minutes."

"And we'll make our withdrawal one minute after that," Cardwell said.

Jacks looked around. "I still can't believe those deputies aren't somewhere around here," he said.

"If they do show up," Ben Cardwell said, "we'll make them sorry they did."

18

Thomas Shaye was checking hotels at one end of town, while James was checking rooming houses at the other. Dan Shaye was still in his house. When Ben Cardwell and Simon Jacks entered the bank, none of the Shaye men were anywhere near it.

Thomas read the name on the register.

"Simon Jacks," he said, looking at the clerk. "Says here he arrived yesterday."

"That's right, Deputy."

"What kind of man is he?"

The clerk shrugged. "Normal, I guess. Not a fancy man, doesn't look like a hard case."

"What does he look like?"

A shrug again. "A salesman, maybe?"

"He have a drummer's case, samples, anything like that?" Thomas asked.

"No."

"Was he wearing a gun?"

"Well, sure."

"What kind?"

"I'm a desk clerk, Deputy," the man said. His name was Hubert Holt, and he was about thirty.

"You been alive long enough to see guns, Hubert," Thomas said. "Old or new?"

"Looked old."

"Clean?"

"I guess."

Thomas closed the register and pushed it back at Hubert. "Where is he now?"

"He left early."

"Okay," Thomas said, "thanks."

He started for the door, then turned back.

"Hubert?"

"Yes, sir?"

"Did he just leave, or did he check out?"

"Oh, he checked out," the clerk said. "Paid his bill and all."

"Okay, thanks."

Thomas left the hotel, stopped just outside. Jacks didn't sound like much, but he'd checked three hotels and this was the only stranger he'd found. He wondered how James was doing.

That's when he heard the shots.

James had checked three rooming houses and come up empty. He was on his way to the fourth when he heard the shots, which sounded like they were coming from the center of town. One shot wouldn't have carried, but there was a volley.

He started running.

* * *

Shaye had left his house and was walking toward the center of town when he heard the first two shots. Immediately, he thought of the bank, and that made him think of the Bank of Epitaph, a year ago.

"No," he said, "not this time."

He took off at a dead run.

Moments earlier Cardwell and Jacks had walked into the bank as soon as it opened. Nancy Timmerman was still in the manager's office, where Fred Baxter was telling her he thought she deserved more responsibility.

Cardwell and Jacks entered and immediately drew their guns.

"Nobody move," Cardwell said to the employees. "First person who does dies."

That's when Baxter came running out of the office, holding a gun.

19

Cardwell had taken into account the fact that the bank was in the center of town. His men were spread out in front so they could handle trouble from any direction. Two of them saw Dan Shaye running toward them, the early morning sun glinting off his badge, and they opened up on him. One bullet struck Shaye in the hip, made him stagger and fall, but he drew his gun as he did so and fired back.

James came running from the same end of town as his father. He'd had a longer run, and when he got there, he saw that his father was down but was firing.

"Pa!"

He drew his gun, ran to where his father was kneeling on the ground. He fired two shots of his own, then grabbed Shaye and dragged him behind a horse trough.

"Pa? You hit?"

"Yeah, I'm hit, James," Shaye said, the pain plain in his voice.

"Bad?"

"Can't tell yet," Shaye said.

The robbers were still firing, keeping them pinned down. Shaye assumed that the first two shots he'd heard had come from inside the bank. There were no more shots from there.

"James, where's Thomas?"

"Other end of town, Pa, checking hotels," James said. "He should be here soon."

"Gotta warn him—" Shaye said, but then there were shots from another quarter, and he knew they were too late.

Thomas came running onto the scene from the other direction, and was immediately fired upon. The shots flew uselessly around him, and he took cover immediately behind a bunch of barrels in front of the hardware store. From where he was, he could see the bank but not his brother or his father. He returned fire, but a barrage from three other men forced him to duck back down behind the barrels. From the writing on them, he knew the barrels were filled with nails. They were plenty good cover against the fusillade of shots being laid down at him.

He knew his father and brother would either hear the shots and come running or had already done so. He could hear other shots beyond the bank when the men stopped firing at him. Apparently, his father and James were in the same situation he was.

"There were other shots bein' fired," James said to his father once all the shooting had stopped for the moment.

"Thomas," he said. "James, look around. Has anyone else responded to the shootin'?"

James looked around them, but there were no townspeople coming to their aid. If anyone had heard the shots, they were hiding inside until the danger passed.

"No one, Pa," he said.

"Epitaph all over again," Shaye said.

"What do we do, Pa?"

"Can you see the bank?" Shaye asked. "I assume that's what this is all about."

James craned his neck. "I can see the front door."

"James," Shaye said, "if there are men inside the bank, we can't let them leave—whether it's with money or a hostage, or both."

"Nancy," James said, rising into a crouch.

"Don't do anything stupid, son," Shaye said.

"We can't do anything at all, pinned down like this," James complained.

"We can see the door," Shaye said. "That's something."

James looked at his father, saw the blood on his hip and thigh.

"How bad are you hit, Pa?"

"I think the bullet took a chunk out of my hip and kept on goin'," Shaye said. "It's not bad, but it would help if we stopped the bleeding."

"Let me shift you back a little so you can watch the bank entrance, and then I'll see about that."

He gripped his father beneath his arms and moved him just a bit, then removed his bandanna and tried to plug the wound. He needed his father's bandanna as well, but eventually got the bleeding under control.

"Hurt?" James asked.

"A lot," Shaye said.

"I wonder why they're not shootin' anymore," James said.

"We're not tryin' to move," Shaye said, "and Thomas probably isn't either."

James looked at his father. "Or he's . . ."

Jacks looked out the front window. One of his men saw him, waved, and used sign language to fill him in on the situation.

"What's goin' on?" Cardwell demanded.

"Looks like our boys have got the law pinned down," Jacks said, turning to look at Cardwell. There were four sacks at the man's feet, all filled with money. On the floor in front of the manager's office was the foolish manager, who had come running out holding a gun. Cardwell had gunned him down immediately, and the manager fired a couple of harmless shots as he went down.

"What about the law?"

"Best I can figure," Jacks said, "they might have an angle on us." He moved to another window. "Looks like they're on both sides, under cover."

"What about Davis? With the horses?"

Jacks peered both ways. "I can't see the horses."

"He might have them in an alley," Cardwell said.

Jacks turned to face Cardwell fully. He had his gun in his hand and his hand at his side. The other employees were grouped in one corner of the bank.

"Your call, Ben," Jacks said.

"Take these money bags over to the door," Cardwell said. "I'm thinkin'."

Jacks came over and dragged the canvas bags over to the door. Cardwell walked over to where the bank employees were grouped. There were four of them, two women and two men, and they all looked frightened.

"Is there another way out?" he asked. "Side door? Back door?"

When there was no answer, he raised his gun, cocked the hammer back, and pointed it at one woman.

"I'm only gonna ask one more time."

20

"Pa?"

"Yes, James?"

"There's a back door to the bank," he said. "It leads to the manager's office. If I can get to it—"

"You have to cross the street to get to it, don't you?"

"Yes, sir," James said. "I can use the alley across the way."

"They'd cut you down before you got across the street."

"But they can also get out that way."

"Where would they come out?"

"That depends," James said. "They have access to two alleys, one on either side of the bank building. If they come out this way, we'll see them. If they come out the other way, Thomas will."

They had both decided, without speaking, that Thomas was still alive and pinned down on the other side.

"Cardwell probably put this whole thing together," Shaye said, "but he apparently forgot one thing."

"What's that?"

"His men may have us pinned down," Shaye said, "but we have them pinned down too."

"Why would he make a mistake like that?"

"Two reasons," Shaye said. "Firing shots inside the bank was not part of the plan, and we've been alerted too early."

"And the second reason?"

"Maybe it wasn't a mistake."

Thomas listened to the quiet. He was waiting to hear something—anything—helpful. Voices from the bank, or the voices of his brother or father. He wondered if he should call out to them or maintain his silence. He peered up over the barrel he was using for cover. He saw two men watching for him, but they didn't fire. He looked past them to see if he could spot his father or brother, but the street curved slightly as it passed the bank, and that's where they must have been.

He could see the bank, though, and nothing was happening there. He didn't know the bank layout well, so he didn't know if there was another way out. He knew James would know, though, since he'd spent so much time in the bank trying to get up the courage to talk to Nancy Timmerman. Then he felt bad for his brother, who must have been worried about Nancy.

Thomas looked behind him and then across the

street. He knew no one was going to come to their aid. Just like in Epitaph, the people of Vengeance Creek were going to do nothing to try and stop the bank robbery.

Now he felt bad for his father, who must certainly have been thinking, Not again.

Cardwell came back from the manager's office, stepping once again over the two bodies that blocked the doorway.

"There's a door back there, all right," he said to Jacks, who was holding his gun on the employees.

"Where does it lead?"

"I opened it and looked out. We can make it to either side of the building."

"Now if we only knew where Davis put the horses."

"He was supposed to be ready to bring them around as soon as we needed them," Cardwell said. He hadn't wanted the horses to be right in front of the bank. That would have been a dead giveaway— but now it would have been convenient.

"We'll have to go out and check both alleys," Cardwell said. "Hopefully, there won't be any law in either one. Our boys will still have them pinned down."

"And be pinned down themselves."

"At least that part is goin' accordin' to plan," Cardwell said.

"So would this part, if you hadn't shot those people."

"He came out holdin' a gun," Cardwell said. "What was I supposed to do?"

"Never mind," Jacks said. "Let's just get out of here. Which one of these folks should we take with us?"

"None," Cardwell said. "A hostage will just slow us down."

"But . . . they'll raise the alarm as soon as we go out the back door," Jacks said.

Cardwell looked at the knife on Jack's gun belt and said, "No they won't."

"It's too quiet," Shaye said. "We've got to do somethin'."

"Can you walk?" James asked.

Shaye tried to move his leg, but the right one wouldn't work for him. The pants leg was soaked with his blood, and the leg itself felt numb.

"No."

"Then I'll have to make a run for it, Pa," James said. "If I can get down that alley, I can make it to the back door."

Shaye grabbed his son's arm. "You've got to be careful, James," he said. "If they know about the back door—"

"I know, Pa," James said. "I might run right into them."

"Help me get into position to lay down some cover for you," Shaye said. "I wish I had my damn rifle."

Once again James placed his hands beneath his

father's arms and dragged him to a new position. The move caused the bleeding to start in his hip again, but he hid that fact from his son.

"Okay," Shaye said, "this is good. I can pull myself up and lay down some fire."

"Do you want my gun, Pa?"

Shaye thought it over. He'd be able to cover his son better with two guns, but that would leave James without a weapon when he reached the back of the bank. There was no point in that.

"No," he said, "you're gonna need it."

"I wonder what Thomas is doin'?" James asked.

"Thinkin'," Shaye said, "just like we are. Maybe when he hears my shots, he'll fire as well."

"I wish we could see him from here."

"So do I, James," Shaye said.

They both hoped that Thomas was all right, but neither voiced that concern.

Shaye reached up with one hand to grasp the horse trough, preparing to pull himself up.

"Ready?" he said to James.

"I'm ready, Pa."

"Okay," Shaye said. "Go!"

21

Rather than fire off his six shots as quickly as possible, Shaye tried to place the shots to give his son the maximum amount of cover. As James began his dash across the street, the two shooters stood up and prepared to fire. Shaye ignored the pain in his hip—while his leg was numb, the hip seemed to pulse with fire—and fired two deliberate shots. He saw one man jerk back as if hit, and the other duck back down. Having located them, he placed his next four shots very carefully, but one of the men was still able to get off a couple of shots at James, which missed.

As Shaye watched, James disappeared into the alley.

When Thomas heard the shots, he had no way of knowing who was shooting. However, he decided to add to the confusion and possibly make a move at the same time. He'd already decided that he could make a run for an alley that ran alongside the bank building, but with no one to lay down cover for him, he knew he would have to do it himself.

He was still trying to decide when more shots came. Impetuously, he stood up and began firing and running at the same time.

Cardwell checked one alley while Jacks checked the other.

"No horses," Cardwell said.

"Same here," Jacks said. "That goddamn Davis!"

They were each carrying two bags of money. From the front of the bank they heard the sound of shots.

"Look," Cardwell said, "we can work our way down the street behind some more of these buildings, maybe even come out on a side street."

"Might as well," Jacks said. "There's nothin' more for us to do here. But when I see Davis, I'm gonna kill him."

"Not if I kill him first."

James stopped in the alley long enough to check himself for bullet holes. When he found none, he continued down the alley with his gun drawn. He inched his way around to the back of the building, being careful in case the bank robbers decided to come out the back door. When he was sure it was safe, he made his way to the door, tried the knob and found it unlocked. He was about to open it when someone came out of the alley on the other side of the building. He turned, gun at the ready. . . .

Thomas also made his way carefully down his alley, watching the mouth of it behind him, in case the shooters decided to follow him. Reaching the end of the alley, he peered around and saw his brother at the back door. He stepped out of hiding, and James turned quickly toward him, pointing his gun.

"Whoa, James! It's me."

James lowered his gun. "Thomas, you okay?"

"I'm fine," Thomas said. "You?"

"Okay, but Pa's hit."

"How bad?"

"Don't know," James said. "He took a bullet in the hip. He's says it kept going, though."

"Well, let's get inside, then, and see what's goin' on so we can get him to a doctor. Did you know about this door?"

"Yeah, I did."

"I didn't," Thomas said. "Thought I'd take a chance, though. Is it unlocked?"

"Yes."

"We better go in before we get company back here."

"I was about to."

"After you, little brother," Thomas invited. "Just be ready for trouble."

* * *

Out front, Shaye reloaded and continued to fire. He didn't want the robbers trying to follow James down the alley. He didn't hear any shooting, though, other than his and their return fire. He hoped that Thomas had acquitted himself well.

He also hoped his boys could get him out of his present predicament, before he bled to death.

James opened the door and stepped in, with Thomas close behind him. He watched for danger inside the bank while Thomas guarded against danger from behind.

"The office is empty," James said. "Come on."

He moved forward and immediately saw the two bodies lying just inside and outside the doorway.

"Oh no!" he exclaimed.

"What is it?" Thomas asked. He had paused to close the door and wedge a chair beneath the doorknob.

"Oh God, no," James said.

"James?"

Thomas joined his brother and saw the bodies.

"Who—"

"The man looked like Mr. Baxter, the manager," James said.

Thomas hesitated, then asked, "And the woman?"

"That," James said, "is Nancy Timmerman."

Thomas was afraid of that.

22

Outside on the street, the remaining bank robbers sensed something was wrong.

"They must have gotten inside the bank somehow," Ed Hurley commented.

Davis, who had abandoned the horses when the shooting started, said, "We better stick together and get inside that bank."

"There's still one more over there," Joe Samuels said. "The others made it to the alleys."

"If they're inside, where are Cardwell and Jacks?" Davis asked.

Beau Larkin looked around. "We have to make a move before this town wakes up and decides to help the law."

"Hey," Bill Raymond said to Davis. "You were supposed to be holding the horses."

"They, uh, spooked and ran off when the shootin' started. I couldn't hold them."

In truth, he had been holding only two horses,

one for him and one for Cardwell. When he heard the shooting, he tethered the horses a couple of blocks away and came to see what was happening.

"Where's Mendez?" Hurley asked.

"He took one in the chest," Samuels said. "He's dead."

"One less share," Hurley said.

"No shares if we don't get into that bank," Raymond said.

"And if we don't have horses," Larkin said. "Davis, you better go get them. We'll check the bank."

"What about the sheriff?" Davis asked.

"He was hit," Larkin said. "If we make a run for the bank, he can't stop us."

Davis was worried now. Not only about where Cardwell and Jacks were, but what these men would do to him if they found out he only had two horses.

"Okay," Davis said.

"We'll meet you in front of the bank," Samuels said.

"Okay," Davis said. "Go."

"You get goin'," Samuels said, "and don't forget those horses."

Davis knew a threat when he heard it. He turned and ran toward the horses, still unsure about what he was going to do.

Samuels looked at the other men, Raymond, Hurley, and Larkin.

"So what do we do?" he asked. "Just rush the bank?"

"That's where the money is," Larkin said.

"Let's do it," Hurley said.

23

"My God!" Thomas said. He had stepped over the bodies and into the bank to check on the other employees. He was shocked to find them all dead, either stabbed or with cut throats.

James was still in the office, kneeling over the prone body of Nancy Timmerman.

"They're dead," Thomas said. "They're all dead."

"Nancy's dead," James said, looking at his brother.

"James," Thomas said, "we know that. We have to be ready for the others outside. And we have to find Cardwell and whoever else was in here."

James stared at his brother, then said, "You better look out the front."

"I barred the back door," Thomas said. "Come on."

James looked down at Nancy again. Thomas reached down and grabbed his brother's arm. "Come on!"

He dragged his brother to the front of the bank in time to see four men charging the door.

"Do we wait for them?" James asked.

"Let's step out and greet them," Thomas said. "That'll surprise them."

James looked back at the bodies of all the employees. He was ready to take some lives.

"Let's do it."

Shaye watched from behind the water trough as the robbers gathered and made their plans. There was nothing he could do about it. He was almost out of bullets, having taken the last of them from his belt, and loaded his gun for the last time. If the men charged him, he was done. If they charged the bank, he could fire six shots in defense of his sons, but that was it.

He knew James and Thomas must be inside the bank by now. Since there were no shots, whichever robbers had been inside must have left. He hoped his boys were smart enough to stay inside.

As he thought that, he saw four of the men step into the street, guns in hand, and charge the bank.

A second later the front door of the bank opened and Thomas and James stepped out.

"Goddamn it!" Shaye said, and pointed his gun.

When Thomas and James stepped through the bank doors, the four rushing robbers stopped short, confused. They hadn't expected the outnumbered deputies to come out and meet them. The moment of hesitation cost them.

"Let's go!" Samuels shouted, but it was too late.

As the four men began running again, Dan Shaye dragged himself out from behind the horse trough and fired at them. His first shot caught Larkin in the side, spinning him around and depositing him on the ground. His second shot finished the man.

Thomas fired once and the bullet went straight into Ed Hurley's heart.

James and Bill Raymond fired simultaneously. Raymond's bullet went wide and smashed a window on the door behind James, while the deputy's bullet hit Raymond in the shoulder, completely stopping his forward progress. It was Thomas who finished him with another heart shot.

Three of the bank robbers were now dead in the street, and the fourth, Joe Samuels, dropped his gun and put his hands in the air.

"Don't shoot! Don't shoot! I give up!"

James aimed his gun at the man and would have shot him if Thomas hadn't grabbed his arm.

"We need one of them alive, James," he said.

James's hand trembled, he wanted so badly to fire.

"Besides," Thomas said, pushing his brother's arm down, "he didn't kill her."

James hesitated, looked at Thomas and said, "Yeah." He holstered his gun.

"Go and get the doc, James," Thomas said. "We need him for Pa."

"But Nancy—"

"Nancy's dead," Thomas said. "Pa ain't . . . yet."

"Yeah," James said. "Yeah."

He took off running down the street toward the doctor's office.

Thomas turned and saw several men—town fathers, all of them—running toward him with an assortment of handguns and rifles.

"Can we help, Deputy?" one of them asked.

"Now?" Thomas asked them. "It's all over and now you want to know if you can help?"

"Hey, we—uh, we had to get our guns, and, uh—" another stammered, but Thomas cut him off.

"Two of you go and take my—take the sheriff to his office. He's been hit."

"Right."

"The rest of you collect the guns from the street," Thomas said. "I'll take the prisoner and put him in a cell."

"What about the bank?" another man asked.

"The money's gone," Thomas said, "and there's no one left alive in there."

The remaining men—town fathers, merchants, men who had helped to build the town and run it—exchanged glances, and then one of them asked, "The money's gone?"

24

When Sean Davis reached the place he'd left the horses, they were gone. That's when he had the first inkling that he might be in trouble. He never could have explained to the other men why he had only two horses—how could he now explain he had none? Then, when he heard all the shooting, he turned and ran back toward the bank. When he got there, he saw that the others had taken the worst of the gun battle with the lawmen, and he knew he had to get out of there. He had to get out of town, and for that he needed a horse.

He stopped wondering who had taken his two horses—his and Ben Cardwell's—and went to find himself just one.

Thomas came out of the cell block, and found his father with his pants down, lying on his desk, and the doctor leaning over him. James was leaning against the wall across the room, his arms folded across his chest, staring at nothing.

"Thomas—" Shaye said, but he was interrupted when the door opened and Mayor Timmerman walked in.

"Shaye!" the mayor shouted. "What are you doing about finding the men who robbed the bank?"

"Mayor—" James said, but stopped when the mayor looked at him.

"Mayor, have you been inside the bank?" Thomas asked.

"No," Timmerman said, "I came right here when I heard it had been robbed."

"Are you concerned about your daughter's welfare?"

"Of course I am," Timmerman said, "but I'm the mayor, I have to be concerned for the town—"

"Mayor . . ." Thomas said.

"What is it, Deputy?"

Thomas looked over at his father, who, with pain etched on his face, nodded for him to go ahead.

"Let's take a walk over to the bank," Thomas said.

"I want to talk to the sheriff."

Thomas took the mayor's arm. The bigger man appeared surprised by the contact.

"My father took a bullet tryin' to save the bank from bein' robbed," Thomas said. "The doctor is workin' on him. You can talk to him later, after we've gone over to the bank."

"Well . . . all right, then," Timmerman said. "I've got to find out how much was taken, anyway. Baxter can tell me that."

"Mr. Baxter is dead," Thomas said, leading the mayor to the door. "He was killed during the robbery. In fact, Mayor, everyone in the bank was killed."

"What?"

Thomas opened the door and ushered the man out of the office.

"That sonofabitch!" James said. "He's more worried about the money than he is about his daughter."

"How is his daughter?" Doc Simpson asked without looking at James. "Are they gonna need me at the bank after I finish stitchin' up your pa?"

"Didn't you hear what my brother said, Doc?" James said. "They were killed. Everyone who worked in the bank was killed."

Now the doctor did look at James. "Everyone?"

"Yes."

"You mean. . . ."

"Yes," James said. "Nancy Timmerman was killed too."

The doctor held James's eyes for a moment, then bent back to the task at hand.

"I should go over in any case," he said. "After all, I'm also the coroner."

"Suit yourself, Doc," James said. "Just finish sewing my pa up first."

"That's what I intend to do, Deputy."

By the time Sean Davis had stolen a horse, he realized what had happened. Cardwell had double-crossed him. He and Jacks had taken the horses and left town with the money. Cardwell had never intended to give him a share, just like he didn't intend to give the others any. He was just as disposable to Ben Cardwell as those other men.

Jesus, Cardwell and Jacks would probably have killed him if he'd met them with the horses, like they had planned.

As Davis rode out of town he vowed that Cardwell was not going to get away with this. And he wasn't going to get away with all the money either.

Ben Cardwell and Simon Jacks stopped riding about a mile out of town, turned and looked back.

"Doesn't look like anyone's comin' after us yet," Jacks said.

"It's gonna take them a while to even realize we were there and gone," Cardwell said. "There are no witnesses in the bank, and my guess is those Shaye lawmen took care of Davis and the others."

"You better hope they did," Jacks said, "or they'll be after us, as well as the law."

"Whoever comes after us," Cardwell said, turning in his saddle, "it ain't gonna be for a while."

They each had two money bags slung over their saddles.

"Maybe we should split up," Jacks said. "We got two bags each."

"We ain't splittin' up," Cardwell said. "There ain't the same amount of money in these bags, Jacks."

Jacks turned around in his saddle and looked at Cardwell. "You think I'd try to cheat you, Ben?"

Cardwell smiled and said, "I just don't want no mistakes made, is all, Simon."

"We better ride, then," Jacks said. "Let's put some miles between us and that bank. That town's gonna be up in arms when they find all them dead people."

"They weren't exactly up in arms when we was robbin' the bank and killin' them people."

"Well, there's still Shaye and his deputies," Jacks said. "Remember, they hunted down the Langer gang and killed most of them."

"A gang leaves a clear trail, Simon," Cardwell said. "We're just two men, and we're gonna split up after we divvy the money. Besides, the way you tell it, that was personal. Ain't nothin' personal about this bank robbery."

"Considerin' what Dan Shaye and his sons did to the Langer gang," Simon Jacks said, "I guess we better hope you're right."

25

"James!"

Shaye looked at his son's back while James stared into the cell block at the surviving bank robber.

"Yeah, Pa?"

"Stop thinkin' about her, son," Shaye said. "It ain't gonna bring her back."

James turned his head and looked over his shoulder at his father. "I know that, Pa."

"Close that door and come over here so we can talk."

James did as he was told, closing the door to the cell block and then walking over to the desk. His father was sitting in his office chair, leaning over to one side to keep weight off his injured hip. He was wearing only his shirt, and was naked from the waist down. The doctor had cut his pants off him, and they were useless.

"James, I hate to give you an errand like this, but I need you to go home and get me a pair of pants. I can't talk to the mayor and the townspeople like this."

"That's okay, Pa," James said. "I need somethin' to do, anyway."

Shaye had painfully donned a fresh pair of trousers by the time Thomas returned with not only the mayor, but other members of the town council. James had resumed his position leaning against the far wall with his arms folded.

Timmerman's face was ashen, and he was not the spokesman for the group, which was odd. Instead, the owner of the general store, Al Donovan, took the lead.

"Sheriff," Donovan said, "we need to know what you're going to do about catching these men."

"We killed three of them, Al," Shaye said, "and we have a fourth in a cell. We don't know how many there were, all told, and we don't know how many were in the bank. We do, however, have a good idea who two of them were."

He explained to Donovan—and the rest of the council—about Ben Cardwell and Sean Davis coming to town and registering at the hotel.

"Why didn't you arrest them when they arrived?" Donovan asked.

"I can't arrest two men for bein' strangers, Al," Shaye said.

"You should gave done something!" Mayor Timmerman said.

"We did, Mr. Mayor," Shaye said. "We watched them."

"Apparently," Donovan said, "you didn't watch them long enough."

"I don't see that I can argue with that, Al."

"Mr. Donovan," Thomas said, "my pa took a bullet tryin' to stop this robbery."

Donovan looked at Thomas. "We appreciate that fact, Deputy," he said, "we really do, but we need to know what's going to be done now!"

"I'm going to interrogate the prisoner," Shaye said, "find out how many men were involved. He should be able to tell us who was in the bank, and then we'll know who killed all those people." Shaye looked at Timmerman, intending to ask him a question, but thought better of it and addressed himself to Donovan once again. "Do we know how much money they got?"

"Not yet," Donovan said.

Shaye shifted painfully in his chair. "We're gonna be puttin' together a posse, Al. I assume we can count on you and the other members of the council?"

"Uh, well, we're merchants, Sheriff, not gunmen. We wouldn't be much help to you."

"There's strength in numbers," Shaye said.

"I'm sure you can find some young men from town who'll volunteer for a posse."

"I guess we'll see," Shaye said.

"Besides," Donovan said, "how do you intend to ride with that wound?"

"I'll be leadin' the posse, Mr. Donovan," Thomas said before Shaye could answer.

"You?" Donovan asked. Behind him, Timmerman snorted.

"Do you have a problem with that, Mayor?" Thomas asked.

"No offense, Deputy, but we hired your pa to be sheriff, largely because we wanted the man who had successfully hunted down the Langer gang."

"Thomas is the one who caught Ethan Langer, Mayor," Shaye said. "He's very capable of leadin' a posse."

"And I'll be ridin' along too," James chimed in.

"Both of my sons are good, experienced deputies, gentlemen," Shaye said. "You have no worries on that account."

"Well, fine then," Donovan said.

"I want to talk to the man in the cell," Mayor Timmerman said.

"I'm afraid I can't allow that, Mayor."

"Why not?"

"Because you're not the law."

"I'm a lawyer," Timmerman said. "The man deserves to see a lawyer."

Everyone stared at Timmerman, including his colleagues on the council.

"Mayor," Shaye said, "are you tellin' me that you want to represent one of the men from the gang who killed your daughter?"

Timmerman's eyebrows shot up and his face, so pale before, suddenly suffused with blood.

"Good God, no!"

"Well then, you can't see him," Shaye said. "The best thing for you to do now is go and take care of your daughter, and be with your family. As for the rest of you, just go on about your business and let us get on with ours."

"Sheriff," Donovan said, "you can't—"

"This way out, gents," Thomas said.

"I'll get the door," James said, pushing away from the wall. He opened the door and stood there like a doorman.

"All right," Donovan said, "but keep us informed about what you're doing, Sheriff."

"Don't worry, Al," Shaye said. "You'll be the first to know—all of you."

Thomas ushered the town council out of the office and James closed the door behind them.

"Ow," Shaye said as he struggled to his feet.

"Pa, what are you doin'?" Thomas asked.

"Like I said," he answered, "I'm gonna talk to the prisoner."

"Are you sure you want to do that?" Thomas asked.

"Can you walk?" James asked.

"I may not be able to ride, but I think I can walk," Shaye said. He took a couple of steps, didn't fall down, and said, "See?"

"We'll come in with you," Thomas said.

"No," Shaye said. "You boys go out and ask around, see what you can find out."

"What are we supposed to ask?" James questioned.

"See if anyone saw anything," Shaye said. "There had to be a man somewhere watching the horses the gang meant to use in their getaway. Also, somebody might have seen the men from the bank after they went out the back way. Go to the livery, the hotels, just ask around and find out whatever you can. The smallest detail might be helpful."

"All right, Pa," Thomas said. "But be careful with the prisoner. You're not steady on your feet."

"I'm not goin' into the cell, Thomas," Shaye said. "Just meet me back here in a couple of hours and we'll compare notes."

"When do we start lookin' for posse members?" Thomas asked.

"Do it now, while you're askin' questions."

"How many, Pa?" James asked.

"I don't know," Shaye said. "I'll know better after I talk with the prisoner."

"You think he'll tell you anythin'?" James asked.

Shaye looked at his sons and said, "I think he better."

26

Dan Shaye tested his legs out before entering the cell block. When he was finally sure he wouldn't fall over, he entered, leaving his gun belt on his desk.

The prisoner was lying on his back staring at the ceiling.

"Why don't we start with your name?" Shaye said.

The man didn't answer.

"You know," Shaye said, "your friends killed everyone who worked at the bank. That's a lot of murders, and you're on the hook for every one of them."

That got his attention.

"I didn't kill nobody."

"Doesn't matter," Shaye said, "because you're the one we caught."

Joe Samuels sat up and stared at Shaye. "You can't pin them killings on me!"

"Sure I can," Shaye said, "especially if you don't cooperate."

Samuels thought about that for a while.

"You know," Shaye said, thinking this might clinch him, "one of the people who worked in the bank and is now dead was the mayor's daughter. Needless to say, he's real upset. He just wants somebody to pay."

The man looked at Shaye. "Samuels," he said, "Joe Samuels."

"That's your name?"

"That's right."

"And who were you working for? Ben Cardwell?"

"I guess," Samuels said. "See, we were all recruited by Simon Jacks, and he works with Cardwell.

"Jacks," Shaye said, frowning. "I know that name."

"You should," Samuels said, "if you're any kind of lawman. He's got a rep."

"What about this other fella, Davis?"

"Davis?" Samuels frowned. "That sonofabitch."

"He got away, you know."

"He was supposed to hold the horses," Samuels said. "I'd like to know what happened to that bastard!"

"And what about Cardwell and Jacks?" Shaye asked. "What was the plan?"

"Cardwell and Jacks were supposed to go into the bank, we was supposed to keep people away—especially law."

"So what went wrong?"

"I don't know," the man said. "There were shots from inside and then you and your deputies came running over. We had to keep you pinned down."

"But you were pinned down too," Shaye said. "Didn't that occur to any of you?"

Samuels frowned.

"How was someone supposed to bring the horses over?" Shaye asked. "How were Cardwell and Jacks supposed to come out the front with the money?"

"How the hell am I supposed to know?" the man asked testily. "I don't plan jobs, I just follow orders."

"Well," Shaye said, "sounds to me like you and your compadres were supposed to get caught while Cardwell and Jacks went out the back way."

Samuels frowned.

"See," Shaye said slowly, "they got out the back after killin' everybody, and you were supposed to get caught out front—caught or killed, probably."

It slowly dawned on Joe Samuels, who whispered, "Sonofabitch." He looked at Shaye. "They set us up!" He said it as if he'd just thought of it himself.

"And now that they're gone, and everyone else is dead, you're the one who's gonna go down for it—all of it."

"Hey, no, wait . . ."

Shaye had started to turn around, as if to leave. "What?" he asked.

Samuels got up and came to the front of the cell. He grabbed hold of the bars and his knuckles went white.

"Whataya wanna know?"

"Do you have any idea where Cardwell and Jacks would go after they left here?"

"No," Samuels said. "Jacks never said."

"Well, do you know where Cardwell or Jacks are from?" Shaye asked. "Maybe they'd go back home."

"I don't know nothin' about Cardwell," Samuels said, "but Jacks used to talk at night. . . ." He trailed off and stopped, a crafty look coming into his eyes.

Shaye waited, because he thought he knew what was coming.

"What do I gotta do to walk away from this?" he asked suddenly.

"Mr. Samuels," Shaye said, then, "or can I call you Joe?"

"Joe's fine."

"Joe," Shaye said, "to tell you the truth, I don't see any way you're walkin' away from this."

Samuels looked crestfallen. "Then I don't know why I should help you."

"Because if you don't," Shaye said, "Cardwell and Jacks—and maybe even Davis—are gonna walk away from it . . . with all that money."

27

James questioned people in the area around the bank while Thomas went to the hotel where Cardwell had stayed, and spoke not only to the owner of the livery, but people who worked in that area. The brothers joined up in the center of town, across the street from the building where the mayor had his office.

They compared notes and realized that they had a few things to tell their father, and that they probably shouldn't waste any time telling it.

"The posse," Thomas said, as if James had reminded him. "How many men did you get?"

"None," James said.

"That's what I got."

"I can't believe this town is just like Epitaph."

"Pa tried to explain it to us after we left Texas," Thomas said. "People hire someone to uphold the law, they think that's it, they're done. Why should they lift a finger when somebody's getting paid to do it?"

"It's their money that was taken from the bank," James said. "You'd think they'd want to do somethin' about gettin' it back."

"And all those dead people," Thomas said. "Their neighbors."

"I never seen anything like that before," James said. "How could a man do that, just butcher a bunch of helpless people?"

"It was quiet," Thomas said. "They probably didn't want any more shots comin' from the bank."

"You know, I don't care about the money," James said. "I just want to bring them back to hang for all them killin's."

Thomas knew his brother was more upset about Nancy Timmerman than any of those other people. He was just thankful that James had never gotten up the courage to actually start a relationship with the girl. If he had been courting Nancy Timmerman, he'd now be totally devastated by her death.

"James, I think you should stay here."

"Why?"

"Pa's gonna need you," Thomas said. "He's not gonna be able to get around—"

"I'm comin' with you, Thomas," James said, cutting his brother off, "and there's no way you can stop me."

Thomas decided to leave the point alone. Maybe James would listen to their father after he calmed down a bit.

* * *

"One man," Thomas told his father, "took two horses from the livery just before the shootin' started."

"Only two?" Shaye asked.

"That don't make sense," James said. "There was ... at least six bank robbers, maybe more."

"There were eight," Shaye said, "but at least six of them were not supposed to leave town."

He related to them the conversation he had with Joe Samuels while they were away.

"So we're only gonna be lookin' for two men?" James asked.

"Maybe three," Shaye said. "We don't know what happened to this fella Davis."

"Maybe we do," Thomas said. "One horse was stolen earlier today. Fella didn't even know it was missin' until I started askin' questions."

"Okay," Shaye said, "so Davis brought two horses from the livery, thinkin' that they're meant for him and Cardwell, when they're really meant for Cardwell and Jacks."

"Jacks," Thomas said. "That name sounds familiar."

"Yeah, I thought so too," Shaye said. He was seated behind his desk again, sitting lopsided to keep pressure off his hip. "Apparently he's got a rep, although as what I don't rightly know yet."

"Okay, okay," James said, "so we're lookin' for three men."

"Looks that way," Shaye said.

"Pa," Thomas said, "I was tellin' James I think he should stay behind to help you."

"First of all, did you even get a posse together?"

Both young men looked away, and Thomas said, "Well, no."

"So it may just be you and James, Thomas," Shaye said. "You're gonna need each other, and you might even have to split up to follow separate trails."

James gave his brother a meaningful look, and Thomas simply shrugged.

"Don't worry," Shaye said. "I can get you a couple of other men to ride with you."

"Who?" Thomas asked.

"You'll see," Shaye said. "For now I want you both to do something. One of you go back to the livery, and the other go and talk to the man whose horse was stolen."

"I talked to them already—"

"Do those horses have any identifying marks, or anything that would make make their gait identifiable? Any markings in their hooves? Any—"

"Okay, okay," Thomas said. "I get it. I didn't ask the right questions."

"Well," Shaye said, "go ask them!"

There was a time, Shaye knew, when posses were not so hard to put together. He knew this from personal experience, since in his youth he had been on the other end many times. As the gunman "Shay Daniels," he had been chased through Missouri and Kansas by posses more times than he could count.

He'd been thinking about those days ever since the bank robbery. It was odd, but sometimes he thought things happened just so he would never forget those days long passed.

But he'd been up against it in Epitaph, and now, apparently, it was to be the same in Vengeance Creek. He couldn't sit a horse, but he wasn't about to send his sons out there alone. It may have been only Cardwell and Jacks now, but who knew how many men they'd surround themselves with by the time Thomas and James tracked them down?

He thought there were a couple of men in town he could draft into service, but he knew he would have to get out of the office and go find them. The doctor had sewed him up, wrapped him tight, and suggested—strongly—that he stay off his feet for at least a few days. But that wasn't going to happen.

He stood up, strapped on his gun, and limped from the office.

Thomas and James decided to stick together rather than split their tasks, so they went to the livery first.

"Horses," the liveryman, Ron Hill, said with a shrug. He gestured with the scarred hand of a man who had been around horses for more than twenty years. "Two horses. They weren't mine, so I didn't pay that much attention to them."

"What do you mean, they weren't yours?" Thomas asked. "Did they ride them in?"

"No," Hill said.

"Did they leave them behind?"

"Not here."

"Mr. Hill," Thomas said, "you have to answer my questions a little more clearly that that."

"They didn't buy the horses from me. They bought them somewhere else, then brought them in here."

"Do you know where they bought them?"

"No."

"Which man brought them to you?"

"The same man who came and got them."

That would be Davis, Thomas thought.

"So you can't tell us if there was anything distinctive about them?" James asked.

"That's right."

"But you're supposed to know horses."

"I know my horses," Hill said. "If they had taken any of the animals from my corral in the back, I could answer your questions."

"Where are the horses the other men rode in on?" Thomas asked.

"In my corral."

"Can you show us the stalls the horses were in before the man came and got them?"

"That I can do."

"And then we'd like to see the horses that belonged to the dead men."

"No problem," Hill said. "Come this way."

It took Shaye three times as long as it usually did to walk the distance from the sheriff's office to the store that housed the gunsmith shop. People had come back onto the streets now that the shooting was over, but they avoided his eyes and stepped out of his way. At least they had the decency to be ashamed of the fact that they had been hiding during the robbery.

When he reached the shop, he stopped outside and peered in through the window. He knew from experience how some people liked to leave their past where it belonged—in the past. He fell into that category, and so did the man inside the gunsmith shop. As far as he knew, he was the only person in town who knew that the gunsmith, Ralph Cory, had once gone by a totally different name.

And he was ashamed of what he was about to do.

When the door to his shop opened, Ralph Cory looked up and saw the sheriff limping into his place of business. He knew that meant one of two things. Either the sheriff needed a gun repaired or he'd been recognized.

Not again, he thought. He actually liked this town, after having been in Vengeance Creek for six months, and people were actually beginning to pay him to do what he liked to do. But this had happened a couple times before. Someone would recognize him, tell the local law, and then he'd be asked to leave.

Well, not this time. Six months. This was the longest he'd spent in one place in quite some time, and his shop was beginning to shape up the way he liked it. He was a businessman, a gunsmith, and that's all he was. If the local law accused him of being anything but—well, he was going to fight back this time.

If they wanted him out of Vengeance Creek, they were going to have to carry him out.

29

"Mr. Cory," Shaye greeted the gunsmith.

"Sheriff. What can I do for you today?"

Shaye closed the door tightly behind him, then turned and limped to the counter. Cory knew that the man had sustained a injury to his hip. He could tell by the way he walked and held himself, but he did not comment on it.

"I suppose you heard the commotion earlier today," Shaye said. "Heard that the bank was robbed?"

"I heard that you and your sons killed yourselves four bank robbers."

"That's right," Shaye said, "and we've got one in jail—but three got away, including the two who murdered everyone inside the bank."

"A terrible thing."

"Yes," Shaye said, "it was awful. One of the people killed was the mayor's daughter."

"I'm sorry for his loss."

"Yeah, I am too."

Cory could see the pain etched on the sheriff's face, and despite himself, he grabbed a chair from behind his counter and carried it around to the front.

"You better sit," he said. "I'll put the closed sign in the window. I have a feeling you and I are in for a long talk."

"Thanks for the chair," Shaye said, and lowered himself painfully into it. "Not that long a talk, though," he said over his shoulder.

Cory came back around to his side of the counter. From beneath it he took two shot glasses and a half-filled bottle of whiskey. He poured two drinks, then stoppered the bottle and put it back. He pushed one of the glasses over to Shaye.

"Thanks," the lawman said.

They both tossed back their drinks, then looked at each other.

"My sons are about to ride out after the remaining bank robbers," Shaye told Cory. "They tried to get up a posse, but everybody turned them down. I can't let them go out there alone, without guidance."

"They're grown men," Cory said.

"They're not ready," Shaye said, "and I can't go with them. This injury keeps me from sittin' a horse."

"What's that got to do with me?"

"I'd like you to go with them," Shaye said. "You see, I know who you really are."

Cory thought about having another drink, but rejected the idea. That wasn't the answer.

"So if I don't agree to go you'll reveal to the town who I really am?" he asked.

"No," Shaye said. "I admit, that was my plan, to threaten you that way. I mean, right up until I got to the door. But not now."

"So what is your plan?"

"This is it," Shaye said. "Just to ask you to go with them."

"You want me to babysit your sons?"

"They're fine young men," Shaye said. "They can take care of themselves, especially Thomas. He's very good with a gun. Someday he'll be better than me, maybe even better than you ever were."

"But . . ."

"But they don't track," Shaye said, "and you do. It's what you used to do."

"A dozen or so years ago," Cory reminded him.

"Trackin' isn't somethin' you forget how to do, is it?"

"I'm not wanted anywhere, you know," Cory said. "I was never a criminal."

"I know you weren't," Shaye said. "Just a man with a reputation who decided to change his life."

"When did you spot me?" Cory asked.

"As soon as you rode into town."

"And you never said a word? Let me settle here?"

"Why not?" Shaye said. "I know what it's like to want to leave a name behind you."

For a few moments Cory studied the man seated before him.

"You're askin' me to do this."

"Yes."

"Not threatenin'."

"No."

"You could, you know," Cory said.

"I have the feelin' this has happened to you before."

"Many times."

"Would you give in this time, again? Give up your business?" Shaye asked.

"No. When you walked in, I had the feeling it was going to happen all over again, and I wasn't going to give in this time. But this . . . this is . . . different."

Shaye shifted his weight in the wooden chair, which creaked beneath him.

"Look, Mister . . . Cory, I'm sorry that I'm askin' this of you, but I don't see that I have a choice."

"So it would be me and your two boys?"

"One other man," Shaye said.

"How will you convince him?" Cory asked. "Does he also have an old life behind him?"

"No," Shaye said, "but he owes me for this one."

Cory hesitated, then said, "I'll have to think it over."

"That's fair," Shaye said, "but my boys are gonna have to leave tonight, before dusk. If they wait until mornin', the men they're chasin' will have too big a head start."

"Give me . . . an hour."

"Fine."

Shaye struggled to his feet, walked to the door. He opened it, considered turning the sign back around to read "Open," but had a feeling the shop was going to stay closed.

30

Thomas and James tried to look the stalls over without stepping inside. There were plenty of tracks made by the horses, but neither of them could pick up anything distinctive.

After that they had Ron Hill take them out back to look at the horses in his corral.

"Which ones were theirs?" Thomas asked.

"You know anythin' about horses?" the liveryman asked them.

"I do," James said. Thomas had to admit, his younger brother was a better judge of horseflesh than he was. He didn't exactly know when that had happened, but it had.

"Well, then you can pick them out," Hill said, " 'cause they ain't mine."

At first Thomas was going to tell Hill they weren't there to play games, but maybe this would take his brother's mind off other things. He watched as James opened the corral door, entered, and closed it behind him. There were enough horses in the corral—twenty head or so—that he could have been trampled if he wasn't careful, but he moved among them with surprising ease, and just as surprising, they seemed to accept his presence.

"This one," James said, putting his hand on a big bay mare that, even to Thomas's unpracticed eye—and now that his brother had pointed it out—had obviously seen better days.

"That's one," Hill said.

James nodded, examined the horse, then lifted each of the animal's feet to check the bottom. That done, he walked among the animals again and picked out a dappled gray that seemed to be a bit swaybacked. When Hill affirmed that this was, indeed, the other horse, James repeated the inspection and then left the corral and returned to his brother's side, after locating and identifying all the horses the bank robbers had ridden into town on.

"So, what did you find out?" Thomas asked.

"Not much."

"But you looked like you knew what you were doin."

"I didn't," James said. "I guess we better go and find Pa."

James headed off, and a confused Thomas hurried after him.

Shaye's hip was screaming bloody murder by the time he reached the Road House Saloon. When he walked through the front door, he was almost dragging his leg.

"Twice in one week," Al Baker said to him. "What an honor, Sheriff. You lookin' for Thomas?"

"I know where Thomas is," Shaye said.

"What happened to you?" Baker asked as Shaye limped to the bar.

"I think you probably already know."

"Yeah," Baker said, "I heard about the robbery."

"And the murders?"

"Yeah. Uh, listen, I'm, sorry I didn't come to help, but it was all the way at the other end of town, and by the time I heard about it, it was all over."

"I'm lookin' for Rigoberto."

"The Mex? What for?"

"I need to talk to him."

"Check the back room," Baker said. "He sleeps back there. I haven't seen him yet this mornin', so he's probably still sleepin' last night off."

"Thanks."

"He's usually up before noon," Baker said as Shaye headed for the back room, "so last night must have been pretty bad."

Great, Shaye thought, the one day he might need Rigoberto Colon, and the man was sleeping off a good one.

Rigoberto Colon was another man in town about whom he knew something nobody else did.

People tended to think town drunks had always been town drunks, but that wasn't the case with Colon. In Mexico, Colon had been part of an aristocratic family, until his father lost all their money and committed suicide, taking Rigoberto Colon's mother, brother, and two sisters with him. Colon happened to be out that day, and so had survived the day's massacre. Since then that was all he had done—survive, rather than live. He wandered from town to town, eventually left Mexico and wandered through Texas and New Mexico until he found his way to Arizona. Around that time he decided he could not deal with the guilt anymore, and crawled into a bottle. He'd been there ever since.

Shaye entered the back room and heard snoring. It was dark, and while his eyes adjusted, he followed the sound and found the sleeping Colon.

"Rigoberto."

The man didn't move.

"Berto!"

This time he followed with a kick to the ribs, not hard, but enough to wake up most sleeping men. Unfortunately, Rigoberto Colon was no normal sleeping man.

"Damn it," Shaye said.

By this time his eyes had adjusted to the dimness of the room. He located a bucket and took it to the back door. He went outside, walked to a horse trough, filled the bucket, and brought it back into the room. He stood above Colon and upended the bucket, pouring the contents over the Mexican's head.

Colon came to with a roar and then a sputter. He was sleeping on the floor, so when he rolled over he simply traveled across the floor a few feet before coming to a stop and sitting up.

"Wha—Who—*Hijo de un carbon*—"

"Wake up, Berto!" Shaye shouted.

The man looked up and squinted at Shaye through the gloom. "Señor Shaye?"

"That's right, Berto," Shaye said.

Colon looked down at himself, then back up at Shaye again with a confused look on his face.

"*Que pasa?*" he asked. What happened?

"I needed to wake you up," Shaye said, showing the Mexican the empty water bucket. "You were sleepin' pretty good."

"I am all wet."

"Well," Shaye said, "get dry and I'll buy you some breakfast. Meet me out front. I have a proposition for you."

As Shaye passed the bar on the way out, Baker asked, "Did you find him?"

"He'll be along," Shaye said. "Don't give him anything to drink."

"Whatever you say, Sheriff."

"I mean it."

Baker put both hands up in a gesture of surrender and said, "I gotcha, Sheriff."

Shaye went outside to wait for Colon.

* * *

Rigoberto Colon wolfed down a plate of steak and eggs while he listened to Shaye's proposition.

"I owe you much, señor," Colon said when Shaye was finished, "but . . . why me? I am but a humble *borracho*."

"That may be so," Shaye said, "but you were not always a drunk, Berto. When you're sober, you're a dead shot, and you can track."

"Si, that is true," the Mexican said, "but I am drunk now."

".I think," Shaye said, "what you need is a reason not to be."

Colon washed down a mouthful of food with a huge swig of coffee, then pushed the plate away from him.

"Perhaps you are right, señor," he said, "but what would this reason be? Money, perhaps?"

"Perhaps," Shaye said, "but I was thinkin' more of this—if you let my sons get killed, you will live to regret it."

Colon thought a moment, then said, "*Sí*, I can understand where that would be a *muy bien* reason, señor."

Shaye leaned forward and looked at the man intently.

"However," he said, "I'd rather you do this because I'm askin' you, Berto, and because you owe me."

Colon sat back in his chair and heaved a great sigh.

"*Sí,* señor," he said, "but I will need a gun, and a horse, and I will need—"

"I'll get you everything you need, Berto," Shaye said. "What I need is you, to help back up my sons. Do we have an agreement?"

He extended his hand across the table.

"*Sí,* señor," Colon said, accepting the hand and shaking it, "we have a bargain."

31

Shaye considered giving Colon some money to buy supplies, but decided not to risk it. The Mexican might just go and spend it on whiskey. Instead he took him to a nearby bathhouse, paid for him to have a bath, then told him to come to the office when he was finished.

"Don't make me come lookin' for you, Berto," he added.

"No, señor," Colon said, dreading the bath, "I will not."

Shaye left him there and went back to the sheriff's office, to find his sons waiting for him.

Shaye listened while his sons related to him the events of the past hour or so.

"So we really couldn't see anything unusual about the horses' tracks in the stalls," Thomas said, "and James looked over their horses and couldn't find anything."

"Did they have the same brand?"

Thomas and James exchanged a glance. James had lifted the horses' legs to inspect the hooves because he thought he might see something there, but neither brother had inspected the brand on either horse. Shaye knew this from the looks on their faces.

"Okay, it doesn't matter," Shaye said. "You have to get on the trail or it's gonna be too cold to follow."

"When should we leave, Pa?" Thomas asked.

"Within the hour. Get yourselves outfitted to spend a lot of time on the trail. You both remember last time."

"Yes, Pa," James said. "We remember."

"Pa," Thomas said, "we don't have a posse."

"I got you some help."

"You did?" James said.

"Who did you get?"

The door opened at that moment and the gunsmith, Ralph Cory, entered. He was carrying a rifle, saddlebags, and was wearing a gun belt.

Thomas and James both looked at their father expectantly.

"Boys, this is Ralph Cory," he said. "Cory, my sons—and deputies—Thomas and James."

Thomas approached Cory with his hand out. "I'm Thomas. You're the gunsmith, right?"

Cory shook hands, looked past Thomas at Shaye for a moment, then said, "That's right."

Obviously, he'd expected Shaye to have told his sons who he really was by now.

"Glad to meet you."

James also shook hands with Cory.

"Is this what you meant when you said you got us some help?" Thomas asked Shaye, then said to Cory, "No offense."

"None taken."

"Yes," Shaye said, "Mr. Cory and one other man."

"One more?" James asked. "Four of us?"

"Better than just the two of you," Shaye said.

"Pa," Thomas said, "we can handle this."

"Thomas," Shaye said, "what were the brands on those horses again?"

Thomas looked down and James looked away.

"Who's the second man?" Cory asked.

"He should be here in any minute," Shaye said. "His name is Rigoberto Colon."

"The drunk?" Cory asked.

"Rigoberto, Pa?" Thomas asked.

"Sober, he's a good man."

"When is he sober?" James asked.

"He knows horses," Shaye said, "and he can handle a gun."

"And what does Mr. Cory bring to the table?" Thomas asked.

Cory left it to Shaye to answer.

"Cory can track," Shaye said, "and he can handle a gun."

There was an awkward moment, then James said, "Well, it sounds good to me. The sooner we hit the trail, the better."

"James," Shaye said, "I'd like you to take Mr. Cory over to the livery and show him the stall where the horses were. Also, show him the horses the bank robbers left behind."

"Yes, Pa."

"Answer whatever questions he has," Shaye added. "Fill him in. And get him a horse. Tell Hill the town will pay him."

"Yes, sir."

"Thomas. . . ."

"Yes, sir?"

"Ribogerto is going to have to be outfitted. Clothes, gun, horse . . . take him and get him whatever he needs. Tell the merchants the town will pay."

"Yes, Pa."

"Be back here by three. You should have enough light left to pick up the trail . . . don't you think, Ralph?"

Cory nodded. At that moment the door opened and a clean, wet-haired Rigoberto Colon walked in, looking sheepish.

"Berto, that's Ralph Cory. He'll be goin' along."

"The gunsmith, *es verdad*?"

"That's right."

"*Con mucho gusto*," Colon said, shaking the man's hand.

"Berto, these are my sons, Thomas and James. Thomas is gonna take you and buy you what you need."

Thomas walked over to Colon, shook his hand and asked, "Shall we go?"

"*Bien*," Colon said. "I am ready. Lead the way, Tomas."

"Thomas, when he's outfitted, take him to the livery and show him what we have as well—and get him a horse."

"Yes, Pa."

As they left, Cory said to Shaye, "Can I talk to you for a minute?"

"Sure."

James looked from his father to the gunsmith and back, then said, "I'll just wait outside."

After James left, Shaye asked, "What's on your mind, Cory?"

"You haven't told your boys who I really am."

"No."

"Why not?"

"I thought that would be up to you," Shaye said. "All they have to know is that you're willin' to help. The rest is your business."

Cory studied Shaye for a moment, then asked, "What about the Mexican?"

"What about him?'

"Is he just a *borracho*? Or is he not who he seems?"

"I guess that'll be up to him to say too, if he chooses."

Cory stared at Shaye for a few more moments, then nodded as if satisfied with the answers he'd gotten and left.

James watched while Ralph Cory studied the ground in the two empty stalls. Standing off to one side, the livery man, Ron Hill, also watched.

"Did you and your brother walk in here?" Cory asked.

"No," James said, "we stayed outside."

Cory started to step into the stall, but remembered that Shaye wanted the Mexican, Colon, to examine them as well. He stepped back and swept the floor of each stall with his eye.

"Do you see anything?" James asked.

"Yes," Cory said, hunkering down in front of one of the stalls, "but it's understandable that you and your brother missed it."

James came over, squatted next to the man and said, "Show me. I want to learn."

Cory looked at James, then said, "All right. Look there." He pointed to a set of tracks. "This horse steps more lightly on his left hind leg."

"Is he lame?"

"No," Cory said, "it's just an odd gait the animal has. Otherwise, it's perfectly sound."

James looked at the man with undisguised admiration.

"Well, I'll be . . ." Hill said, scratching his head. "I never woulda noticed that."

"I don't think my pa would even have seen that."

"Don't sell your pa short, son," Cory said, straightening up. "Take me out to the corral and show me those other two horses."

"Yes, sir. This way . . ."

Thomas and Colon went to the general store and got the Mexican outfitted with saddlebags, blankets, a bedroll, and some new shirts and trousers. With both of them carrying bundles, they walked to the livery to get him a horse and let him have a look at the now empty stalls where the bank robbers' horses had been.

Upon entering the livery they set the bundles aside on a bale of hay, then Thomas showed Colon the stalls.

"*Muy bien,*" the Mexican said after only a moment. "I have seen enough."

"Then let's find Hill and get you a horse," Thomas said. "Must be out back."

The two men went out to the corral, where they found Hill and James watching while Ralph Cory inspected the horses formerly owned by the bank robbers.

"Mr. Hill," Thomas said, "Rigoberto needs a horse."

Hill frowned at Colon and asked Thomas, "He got money for a horse?"

"The town does," Thomas said. "They'll be footin' the bill."

"Go ahead and pick one out, then."

"*Con permiso,*" Colon said. "I will wait for Señor Cory to finish."

"Fine," Thomas said. He walked over to his brother, who quickly told him what Cory had found in the stalls.

"The Mexican said the same thing," Thomas informed his brother.

"He did?" James was shocked. "I guess Pa's right about him not bein' just a drunk."

"We been livin' here as long as Pa has," Thomas said. "How come we don't know these two men?"

James shrugged and said, " 'Cause we ain't Pa."

Cory came waking over to them, remaining inside the corral. "Double W brand," he said. "Know it?"

"Never heard of it," Thomas said.

"Me neither," James said.

"Maybe your old man has," Cory said. "You buyin' the Mexican a horse?"

"Yes," Thomas said, "but he's—"

"That claybank over there looks good," Cory said, "but I expect he'll want to pick his own out."

He opened the gate and exited the corral.

"What about you, Mr. Cory?" Thomas asked. "Do you need a horse?"

"I have my own, thanks," Cory said. "Did the Mexican see what I saw in the stalls?"

"Uh, yeah, yeah, he did," James said.

"Good," Cory said, "then he's got a good eye. When are we pullin' out?"

"One hour," Thomas said. "We'll meet back here."

"Fine," Cory said. "I'll see you then."

As the man started walking away James asked Thomas, "Should I go with him?"

"No," Thomas said. "We'll see him in an hour." He turned. "Rigoberto, time to pick a horse."

The Mexican came over and stood next to the two brothers. "I already have, Tomas."

"What, without goin' into the corral to look them over?"

"*Sí,*" Colon said. "I have—how do you say—the eye for horseflesh? I can 'see' what makes a good horse."

"Which horse?" Hill asked.

"The claybank."

"Good choice," Hill said.

Thomas and James exchanged a glance.

33

"Double W?" Shaye asked.

"Yes," Thomas said.

Shaye looked at James.

"We went into the corral and looked after he left," James said. "Two Ws, side by side."

"Intertwined?"

James frowned.

"Connecting," Thomas said to James, and then to Shaye, "No, they weren't. Just side by side."

"Do you know it, Pa?" James asked.

"No," Shaye said, shifting painfully in his desk chair. "No, I never heard of it." He took out his watch and looked at it. "You boys ready to go? You got a couple of hours of daylight left."

"We're ready," Thomas said.

"Just remember," Shaye said, "you're wearing the badges. Listen to what Cory and Berto have to say, and then you make the decisions. Understand?"

"We understand, Pa," James said.

"Pa," Thomas asked, "how far do we go to catch these men?"

Before Shaye could answer, James said, "We go till we catch them, Thomas. They killed Nancy!"

Shaye looked at his sons. The urgency to capture these men and bring back the money was certainly not the same as it had been the year before, when they spent weeks tracking down the Langer brothers and their gang. But Caldwell and Jacks had killed many citizens of Vengeance Creek, including the mayor's daughter, and they certainly could not be allowed to get away with that.

"Thomas," he said. "Do you have any problem with chasin' them until you find them?"

"These badges won't mean much once we leave the county, Pa," Thomas said.

James drew his gun and said, "These guns will mean just as much, no matter how far we have to go."

"Put it away, James," Shaye said. "How many times have I told you not to pull that unless you intend to use it."

"I intend to use it, Pa!" James said fiercely.

"I know you do, son," Shaye said, "but not now, right?"

James looked sheepish, and returned the gun to his holster. "Sorry, Pa."

"James, I know you're upset about Nancy's death, but don't let that cloud your judgment."

"No, Pa," James said, "I won't."

"Don't worry, Pa," Thomas said, "I'll make sure he doesn't."

"I'm counting on the two of you to watch out for each other," Shaye said. "And watch Rigoberto. Don't let him get hold of a bottle."

"What about Ralph Cory?" Thomas asked.

"What about him?"

"Do we have to watch him too?"

"No," Shaye said. "There won't be any reason for you two to watch Cory."

"But he'll be watching us?" James asked.

"He'll be watching your backs," Shaye said, "and you'll be watching his. It'll be up to the four of you to keep each other alive."

"We're only tracking two men, Pa," Thomas said.

"You don't know that," Shaye said. "There's another man floating around somewhere—and you don't know where the other two are headed, or what's waitin' there. So don't assume you're only gonna have to deal with two men."

Thomas nodded and said, "Okay, we'll remember."

"You better get goin'," Shaye said. He grimaced. "I wish I was goin' with you."

"So do we, Pa," James said.

"Be careful, boys."

Thomas moved to the desk before his father could try to rise and held out his hand. Shaye shook it firmly, then followed suit with James. As they left, Shaye thought how proud he was of his two remaining sons—and how he hoped to see them again, soon.

Ralph Cory was standing in front of the livery stable, pulling the cinch on his saddle tight, when Rigoberto Colon came from behind the stable, leading his new animal.

"Ah, Señor Cory," he said. "*Buenos noches*. It seems we are the first to arrive, eh?"

"It seems."

Cory looked at Colon. The man's eyes seemed clear, which was an oddity. Cory had seen the Mexican more than a few times around town and he had always been drunk. He wondered what Sheriff Daniel Shaye knew about the man that would sober him up so quickly and make him so ready to ride out as part of this very small posse.

Colon was chewing on a toothpick and watched as Cory secured his saddle to his satisfaction. The animal itself was a marble-speckled Appaloosa, about fifteen hands high.

"That is a handsome animal, señor," Colon said.

"Thanks."

"What is he? Eight? Nine?"

"Ten," Cory said.

"Ah," Colon said, "he has seen better days, then."

Cory turned and looked at Colon. "Haven't we all?"

Colon smiled, revealing several gold teeth. "*Sí,* that is true, señor. I meant no disrespect to your animal."

"None taken."

"You chose the same horse I did, eh?"

"The claybank won't have the stamina of my horse," Cory said, "but he'll do."

"*Sí,*" Colon said, "he was the best of the bunch." The Mexican caressed the horse's neck. "You also noticed what I did about the horse that was in the stall."

"Light stepping in his left hind, you mean?"

"*Sí,*" Colon said. "The two young deputies, they have much to learn from us, eh?"

"I'm not here to teach them."

"Then why are you here?"

"The same reason you are, I suppose."

"I am here to help capture the bad men," Colon said. "And because I owe Señor Shaye a debt of gratitude."

Cory turned and faced the Mexican. "Then I guess we're not here for the same reasons, are we?"

"I do not know, señor," Colon said with a shrug. "You have not told me your reason."

"Let's just say I didn't have much of a choice."

Colon nodded, then looked down at the gun on Cory's hip.

"That is a fine weapon."

"Nothin' fancy."

"That is what I meant," Colon said. "You can tell when a man cares for his gun, Señor Cory.

Better that it should shoot straight than be adorned with silver and look pretty, eh?"

"It'll shoot straight," Cory said. "I made it myself."

"Would you like to see my gun?"

Cory tensed as Colon drew his weapon, then executed a neat border shift and held it out. It was a Navy Colt, which surprised him. He figured Colon for a fancy gun to match the silver conches on his saddle. He took it, hefted it, inspected it, and handed it back.

"It'll do."

"Ah," Colon said, "I am not known for my shooting, señor, but I too can at least shoot straight—and I can hit what I shoot at."

"With a gun that size," Cory said, "you'd only have to catch a piece of a man to stop him."

"A bullet from this gun," Colon said proudly, "would take a piece of a man right off, eh? An arm, a leg. Whoosh! Gone."

Cory looked at Colon's saddle. "That yours, or did the boys buy it for you?"

"The saddle? She is mine," Colon said, putting his hand on it. "A—how do you say—something from a better time?" He rubbed his hand over the shiny leather. "It is all I own anymore."

Cory recognized that the saddle had once cost a pretty penny. That meant that Rigoberto Colon had come from money at one time.

"Ah," Colon said, looking past Cory, "here

come our two young lawmen. I suspect it is time for us to be on our way."

Cory turned his body sideways so he could watch Thomas and James approach without giving his back to the Mexican. A discussion of horses, saddles, and guns was not enough to bond two men together in trust—not yet, anyway.

34

"It's gettin' dark," Simon Jacks said. "We should camp."

"We'll keep goin' awhile," Ben Cardwell said.

"What for?" Jacks asked. "You think there's a posse out after us? Did you see any of them townspeople try to help the law? They ain't gonna get a posse together, Ben—leastways, not today."

"Maybe not," Cardwell said, "but we'll keep goin' just the same."

"You worried about Davis?" Jacks asked. "Hell, he's probably dead, and if he ain't, he ain't got the balls to come after us."

"Don't sell Davis short," Cardwell said. "If he's mad enough—if any man's mad enough—he'll fight."

"So if he finds us, we kill him," Jacks said. "You were gonna do that anyway."

"Simon," Cardwell said impatiently, "we'll ride a bit longer before we camp. I'm callin' the shots here, not you, remember?"

"Oh, I remember, Ben," Jacks said. "I remember real well."

"Good," Cardwell said, "so let's get a move on."

Jacks followed Cardwell. There was no harm in letting the man continue to lead as long as it suited him. It had served them both well . . . so far.

Sean Davis studied the ground, looking for the odd impression he knew would be left by either Ben Cardwell's horse or Simon Jacks's. One of them was riding an animal that stepped lightly with his rear left leg. It was going to make it easy for him to track them down—at least, one of them—and get his share of the bank money from them.

He knew Ben Cardwell didn't have much respect for him, but he was going to show him and Simon Jacks the error of their ways. Not only had they tried to cut him out his share, but they'd left him behind to be captured, or killed.

He was going to show them how wrong they were.

"You fellas gettin' acquainted?" Thomas asked Ralph Cory and Rigoberto Colon.

"Yeah," Cory said, "just a bit."

"*Un poquito.*"

"We'll just saddle our horses and be right with you," Thomas said. "Come on, James."

The two brothers entered the stable, leaving Colon and Cory behind.

"I wonder why they're comin' with us?" James

asked as they saddled their mounts. "I mean, nobody else in town wanted to volunteer. Why them?"

"I get the feelin' neither of them volunteered either."

"Whataya mean?"

"I mean," Thomas said, pulling the cinch tight on his saddle, "I think they're only doin' it because Pa asked them to."

"Why would they do that?" James wondered. "You think Pa knew them before we came to town?"

"Probably not," Thomas said, "but I think he knows them now."

"Well," James said, "we'll be on the trail with them. Maybe we'll find out just who knows who."

Thomas turned his horse and waited for James to bring his around.

"I don't think they know each other," he said. "They didn't look real comfortable together, out there."

"Think maybe they got money in the bank?" James asked. "That's why they agreed?"

"Rigoberto doesn't look like someone who has money, does he?" Thomas asked.

As they walked their horses to the doors James said, "I never would have picked him for ridin' in a posse either."

"Good point."

When they got outside, Cory and Colon were already mounted.

"Some of these tracks have been trampled," Cory said, "but I think we got a general direction."

"Let's head that way, then," Thomas said. "We're losin' daylight fast."

Cory and Colon exchanged a glance, then looked at Thomas and James.

"Who takes the lead?" Cory asked.

"Let's start with you, Mr. Cory," Thomas said, "and see how it goes from there."

"Okay," Cory said, "and the name's Ralph."

"Lead the way, Ralph," Thomas said. "We're right behind you."

Shaye dragged himself to the door and outside onto the boardwalk. From his vantage point he was able to watch the four riders leave town.

"That's the best you could do?" a voice asked.

He turned and saw Mayor Timmerman standing there.

"I don't see you gettin' on a horse, Mayor," Shaye said, "and it was your daughter they killed."

"Don't be a fool," Timmerman said. "I'd probably wind up getting one of your sons killed."

Shaye leaned against the wall and said, "I hate to admit it, but you have a point there."

"You couldn't get more than four men?"

"This is your town, Mayor," Shaye said. "What do you think?"

"Cowards," Timmerman said sourly. "You know, there was a time people had pride in their town and would rise up and protect it when there was a need."

"Those days are long gone, Mayor," Shaye said. "Now it's up to two green deputies, a gunsmith, and a drunk."

Shaye limped back into the office and closed the door in Timmerman's face.

35

"I can't see a thing," James said.

"Quiet," Thomas said.

Ralph Cory was down on one knee, examining the ground in the waning light of the day.

Rigoberto Colon rode up next to the brothers from his position rising drag.

"Señor Cory has very good eyes," he said. "One would think he once did this for a living, *es verdad*?"

Thomas said, "I don't know . . . maybe."

"What do you see, Rigoberto?" James asked.

"I see nothing from here," Colon said. "It is Señor Cory's job. If he asks for my help, I will look."

James looked up at the sky. It wasn't dark yet, but the moon had replaced the sun in the sky.

"We should camp," he said.

"Wait," his older brother said.

"For what?"

"Pa told us to use Mr. Cory and Berto," Thomas said, "and that's what I intend to do."

"One of you want to step down here?" Cory said then, over his shoulder.

"Sit tight," Thomas said, and dismounted. He walked over to where Cory was still crouched.

"Come on down here," Cory said, and Thomas got down into a crouch. Cory pointed. "See that?"

Thomas leaned forward. "It's the print we've been followin'," he said, "isn't it?"

"Yes," Cory said, "and there." He pointed again. "The horse that's been ridin' with it."

"Slightly longer stride on the right side," Cory said.

"How can that be?" Thomas asked.

"What?"

"Both horses have somethin' unusual about their tracks."

Cory looked at Thomas. "If you have a good eye, no two tracks are alike."

"Yes, but—"

"Look there." The man was pointing in yet a third direction, but still within arm's length.

"What's that?" Thomas asked. "Tracks of a third horse?"

"Very good," Cory said. He reached down and brushed away some debris. "The third horse's tracks have crossed those of the other two."

"Someone else is trackin' them?"

"Apparently," Cory said. "Wasn't there some mention of a third man?"

"Yes, there was. The man who rode into town with Ben Cardwell, originally."

"Looks like maybe he didn't appreciate being left behind."

Cory brushed his hands together and stood up, followed by Thomas.

"What do you suggest we do now?" Thomas asked.

Cory started to answer, then stopped and looked up at James and Colon.

"Ask Señor Colon," he suggested.

"Rigoberto?" Thomas said. "What do you think?"

"If someone is crossing their tracks, we're going to need daylight," Colon said immediately. "I suggest we camp here for the night and get an early start."

Thomas looked at Cory.

"That's what I suggest."

Thomas looked at James, said, "We'll camp here."

James let out an exasperated sigh and commented, "That's what I said."

"Then it's unanimous," Thomas said to his brother, "isn't it?"

36

Thomas took control and divided up the labor. Rigoberto look care of the horses. James got the fire going and was in charge of preparing something to eat. Thomas and Cory scouted the general area on foot, just in case.

"If they're close by, they're going to see the fire, or smell what's cooking," Cory said.

"Won't make a difference," Thomas said. "They gotta know we're comin' after what they done, don't you think?"

"I suppose."

"I get the feelin' you more than suppose, Mr. Cory."

"What's that mean, Deputy?"

"Means my pa knows somethin' about you that I don't," Thomas replied, "but I aim to find out what it is."

"How do you intend to do that?"

"Maybe I'll just ask."

"Well," Cory said, "maybe when you do, I'll

just answer. I hear a stream. Think I'll fill all the canteens."

They went back to camp, and when Cory left with the canteens, Thomas stayed.

"We haven't come that far, you know," James said.

"We'll make up some time tomorrow."

"What do we do if Davis catches up to them first?"

"James, we're just gonna get the money back from whoever we catch up to."

"And take them back to Vengeance Creek to hang for killin' Nancy," James added.

"Is that what you want to do?" Thomas asked.

"Whataya mean?"

"I had the feelin' you just wanted to kill them. You know, for killin' your girl and all."

"Thomas, I'm not stupid."

"I never said you were, little brother."

"I know Nancy wasn't my gal," James went on. "Hell, I never said more than two words to her at the bank, and that was when I was makin' a deposit."

Thomas remained silent, even though that was the way he'd had it figured.

"But who knows what woulda happened if I ever did get up the gumption to talk to her?" James finished. "Now I'll never know."

"I understand, James," Thomas said.

"I'll have somethin' for us to eat in a few minutes," James said, dropping some bacon into a frying pan.

"Okay," Thomas said. "I'll pour everybody some coffee."

Cory took his coffee and his plate to a dark corner and ate on his own. Rigoberto Colon also chose to eat alone, but he did so within the circle of the fire.

Thomas and James sat at the fire and ate.

"It feels funny," James said.

"What does?"

"Bein' here without Pa."

"I know," Thomas said, "but Pa's trustin' us to do this, James."

"You think so?"

"I know so."

"Then why send us with them?"

"The more the merrier."

James looked around. "Nobody seems real merry."

"It's just a sayin', James."

"Pa only let us go because he got shot," James said. "If he hadn't, he'd be here with us."

"If he didn't trust us, he never woulda let us go."

"How do you know?"

"Because if he didn't think we could handle ourselves, James, he never woulda sent us out to get ourselves killed."

James looked thoughtful and said, "Hmph, I guess you're right about that."

"Any more of those beans left?" Thomas asked.

"Sure," James said. "You like 'em?"

"Let's just say it's all we've got."

Still later, James leaned back as the brothers were sharing a cup of coffee and asked, "Do you think Pa shoulda deputized them two?"

He looked across the fire at Colon, and still farther away, at where Cory was seated.

"I get the feelin' they wouldn't be here if he'd tried that. They don't seem the badge-totin' type," Thomas said. "I think Pa did what he did to get them to come with us."

"I wish I knew who they really are."

"They seem to know what they're doin'," Thomas said. "That's the important part."

"Aren't you curious, Thomas?"

"Hell, yes, I'm curious," the older brother said. "I practically told Cory I was gonna find out who he really is."

"And what did he say?"

"He told me all I had to do was ask."

James looked surprised. "And did you?"

"No."

"Why not?"

"I didn't feel it was the right time."

"Well, let's go and ask him now," James suggested, sitting up straight.

"Still not the right time, James."

"When will it be the right time?"

Thomas shrugged and said, "We'll know."

* * *

Cory came walking over to the fire and asked, "Any more of that coffee?"

"Sure," James said, reaching for the pot.

"Why don't you drink it here with us, Ralph?" Thomas asked while James filled the cup.

"Sure," Cory said, "why not?" and hunkered down across the fire from them.

"Hey, Rigoberto," Thomas called out. "Come have some more coffee with us."

"But of course," Colon said, and walked over to the fire. "It would be my pleasure."

"You know," Cory said to Colon, "for a drunk, you don't seem to need a drink all that much."

"Who tol' you I was a drunk because I need to be?" the Mexican asked. "We are men, señor. We make decisions in life."

"And your decision was to be a drunk?" Cory asked.

"Just as yours was to be a gunsmith, no?"

Ralph Cory frowned and said, "There was a lot more to it than that, for me."

"Perhaps you will tell us about it?"

"Perhaps," Cory said, "but not right now."

"And these two fine young gentlemen," Colon said, "they decided to be lawmen."

"There was more to it than that for us too," Thomas said.

"The decision kinda got made for us," James said.

"How interesting," Colon said. "Then I am the only one who made up my own mind?"

The other three men stared at him, and then Cory said, "I get the feeling there was more to it than that for you too, Rigoberto."

Colon hesitated, then said, "Perhaps . . . but we are not gathered here to discuss that, are we?"

37

Thomas had given himself the last watch when he outlined it the night before. James went first, then Colon, and Ralph Cory was third. When Cory woke Thomas, he told him that he'd just made a fresh pot of coffee.

"Want a cup before you turn in?" Thomas asked.

"Sure."

They settled in at the fire with a cup each.

"I'm ready," Thomas said.

"Ready for what?"

"To ask you the question."

Cory picked up a stick and poked at the campfire, bringing it flaring to life. "Your Pa really didn't tell you any of this?" he asked.

"Pa didn't tell us anything about you, Mr. Cory," Thomas said. "I guess he wanted us to get to know each other on our own."

"First night out?"

Thomas shrugged. "Curiosity got the better of me."

Cory fell silent.

"Where do you know my pa from?" Thomas asked, figuring the man needed a shove to get started.

"I never knew your pa," Cory said, "but apparently he knew me from somewhere. He recognized me as soon as I moved to town."

"And he told you that?"

"No," Cory said. "He waited until yesterday for that. Waited until he needed me, I guess."

"So what's the big secret?" Thomas asked. "Who are you, really?"

"My real name is Dave Macky."

Thomas frowned because the name sounded familiar—and then he got it.

"Bloody Dave Macky?" he asked. "The bounty hunter who always brought back his man dead?"

"That's a slight exaggeration," Macky said, "but it happened often enough to earn me that nickname. I thought you and your brother might be too young to remember me."

"I only remember stories I heard."

"Everybody heard stories," Macky said. "That's why I was forced into bringing back so many men dead. They couldn't have it any other way."

"Are you sayin' they wanted to die?"

Cory/Macky dropped the stick he'd been using to poke the fire and looked at Thomas.

"I'm saying they all heard the stories about 'Bloody Dave' and figured they either had to fight or die. I told them to drop their weapons and I'd take them back live, but they didn't believe me. They thought I'd gun them down in cold blood once they were unarmed, so they forced the issue."

"So you finally got tired of it?"

"I got tired of the killing, yeah," the man said. "I thought I was doing the right thing, bringing wanted men to justice, but it all changed. Too much killing. I walked away."

"And went where?"

"Wherever I could go where people didn't know me," he said. "I'd use a phony name, try to start a life somewhere, but sooner or later someone would come to town and recognize me."

"Like my pa did."

Macky nodded. "Only he's the only man who kept quiet about it . . . until now."

"He only did it because nobody in town would volunteer for the posse," Thomas said. "Nobody came out to help us when the bank was hit."

"I know," Macky said, looking away. "I . . . I feel bad about that. I started to grab a gun, to come out and help, but I hesitated . . . thought about it too long . . . and then it was all over."

"So that's why you agreed to help?" Thomas asked. "Out of guilt?"

"That's one reason."

"What's the other?"

"Your pa, he gave me the option of saying no, said he still wouldn't tell anyone who I was. How could I say no to that kind of an honest plea?"

"That's Pa," Thomas said. "He's real honest."

"I understand he wasn't always that way."

"He told you that?"

"Yes."

"Just another example of how honest he is, now."

"I realized that," Macky said. "I tried to convince myself to say no anyway, but I couldn't do it."

"So then the stories weren't true?"

"No," Macky said. "Oh, I brought some men in draped over their saddles, but only when they gave me no choice. Soon, though, none of them did."

"So that's why you're such a good tracker?"

"Experience," Macky said. "I tracked so many men that soon it was my strength."

"So you think you can track these men?"

"As long as they don't manage to find some surface that won't show sign."

"Like solid rock?"

"You can track over solid rock," Macky said. "Shod horses, anyway."

"We gotta catch these men, Mister . . . what do I call you? Cory? Macky?"

"Call me Ralph," the man said. "Ralph Cory is the name I'm hoping to go back to after this is all over."

"All right, Ralph."

"I expect you to tell your brother," Cory said. "And Colon, I guess."

"Yes, but I won't tell anyone else, Ralph," Thomas said, "I swear."

"I believe you," Cory said. "I'm sure your brother will keep quiet as well."

"And Rigoberto?"

Cory hesitated, then said, "Go ahead and tell him. I get the feeling he's got some secrets of his own. We all do."

"I don't," Thomas said.

"You and your brother are young," Cory said, getting to his feet. "But you will have secrets, eventually. I'm going to turn in, Thomas."

"Good night, then . . . Ralph," Thomas said. "Thanks for bein' honest with me."

"Seems to be what you Shayes value," Cory said.

Cory rolled himself up in his bedroll, as it had gotten chilly during the night. Thomas poured himself another cup of coffee and dwelled on the fact that he was tracking bank robbers and killers with the famous—and infamous—Bloody Dave Macky.

In the morning, Thomas decided to start the day by introducing James and Rigoberto to Dave Macky. This way, at least they all knew they were riding with a professional.

"I am impressed," Colon said, after "Ralph Cory's" real identity was revealed.

"Don't be," Cory said.

"And what do we call you, now that we know who you are?" James asked.

The answer was the same one Thomas had gotten during the night.

"Just call me Ralph," Cory said. "That's the name I answer to."

"Now that we've got that settled," Thomas said, "let's break camp and get movin'. Ralph, you'll take point again. Berto, you ride drag."

"*Sí, mi jefe.*"

As they collected their gear and saddled their horses, James said to Thomas, "I feel odd."

"About what?"

"Us bein' in charge when we got Bloody Dave Macky riding with us."

"He's not Macky, James," Thomas said. "He's Ralph Cory. Let's try to remember that."

"But Macky, he's a legend."

"Remember what Pa told us about him bein' Shay Daniels?" Thomas asked. "If we allow him to leave that in the past we got to allow Ralph Cory the same thing."

"I can't believe Pa knew about him and never told us."

"Pa doesn't tell us everything, James," Thomas said, "and we don't tell him everything."

As Thomas led his horse away, James called after him, "Hey, what are we keepin' from Pa?"

With the campfire stamped cold, the members of the four man posse mounted up and headed off single file in the direction of the tracks. They rode in silence for some time, each apparently alone with his own thoughts.

About midday Cory called a halt to their progress and once again dismounted to inspect the ground.

"Rigoberto?" he called. "You want to have a look?"

Colon handed the reins of his horse to James, dismounted and walked over to where Cory was crouched.

The two men examined the tracks left by three

horses, exchanged a few words, then stood up and faced the two young deputies.

"We're agreed that we think we'll catch up to the third man before he catches up to the first two."

"That's not who we want," James protested. "He wasn't in the bank when the people were killed."

"If we run him down first," Colon said, "we will not have much choice, Deputy. We cannot just let him go."

"Berto is right, James," Thomas said. "We're gonna have to take them as they come."

"Then will one of us have to take him back to town?" James asked. "I don't want it to be me, Thomas."

"I don't see any reason why we couldn't keep him with us," Cory said, before Thomas could reply. "He might come in handy predicting where the other two might go."

"Why don't we deal with that if and when it happens," Thomas said. "Right now whataya all say we keep movin'."

"You two are in charge," Cory said.

He and Colon mounted up. James handed Colon back his reins, and Thomas did the same for Cory.

"We do have something to secure these men with when we catch up to them, don't we?" Cory asked.

"Um, we can tie them up."

"No chains? Or manacles?" Cory asked.

"Sorry."

"That's okay," the ex-bounty hunter said, patting his saddlebags. "I have my own."

39

Ben Cardwell dumped the remnants of the morning's coffee on the fire and shook out the pot. Simon Jacks came walking over, leading both their horses. At Cardwell's feet were his saddlebags with his share of the money. Jack's saddlebags were already on his horse. They hadn't actually gone through the saddlebags to see how much was in each, because they were on the run, so their split hadn't yet been made. Cardwell wanted to wait until they were someplace safe, and until then they were joined at the hip.

"Ready to go?" Jacks asked.

"Just let me put this coffeepot away," Cardwell said.

While he did that, Jacks took the time to look behind them, around them, and ahead. Nobody was in sight.

"If I was Davis," he said, "I woulda traveled at night to make up some time."

"Not him," Cardwell said. "He hates to ride at night."

"Maybe I should just wait here and ambush him," Jacks suggested. "Get rid of him once and for all."

"Sure," Cardwell said. "Just let me have your saddlebags and I'll take care of the money."

"You don't trust me to catch up to you with the money that's in my saddlebags?"

"Let's just say I trust you more than anyone else, Jacks," Cardwell said, "and the answer is no. When it comes to this much money, I don't trust anybody."

"You know what?" Jacks said. "Neither do I. Why don't we both wait here for him and get rid of him?"

"Because on the off chance that there actually is a posse coming after us," Cardwell said, "we better just keep movin'."

Jacks handed Cardwell the reins of his horse and said, "Okay, so let's go."

Both men mounted up and took the opportunity to look around them again.

"Nothin'," Jacks said.

"For now," Cardwell said, "but I coulda swore I smelled a campfire last night."

"Yeah, me too," Jacks said.

"Bacon?"

Jacks nodded. They had made coffee and beans the night before, and that was all.

"Let's move, Simon," Cardwell said. "Faster

we get to a town, the faster we can split the money."

And go our separate ways, Jacks added to himself.

40

Ben Cardwell and Simon Jacks came to the town of Blue Mesa, Arizona, at around dusk. It was only a few miles from the borders of Colorado and Utah Territory. From there they could go on to either, or they could split up and go their separate ways.

Jacks was having second thoughts about doing that, though. While he had not counted the money in his saddlebags, he knew it was more than he'd ever had at one time before. That was due to Ben Cardwell, and he knew it. Even once they combined the contents of their saddlebags and then split the money in half, he would have more money that he'd ever had before—but was that enough? Apparently, not for Ben Cardwell. He'd been talking for days about this bank he knew of in Colorado.

"You think this is a lot of money?" he'd asked Jacks, tapping his saddlebags. "This ain't nothin'."

Cardwell could be an asshole sometimes, but

for the promise of more money Jacks thought he could put up with it. He liked not having to do any of the planning himself.

"We been ridin' for days," he said as they rode into Blue Mesa. "Is this where we finally count the money?"

Cardwell had refused to count up the money until they could do it in a hotel room, and so far they hadn't passed a town he wanted to stop in.

"This is it," he said, "and then we can either stay together or go our separate ways."

"I think I'd kinda like to see this other bank you been talkin' about," Jacks said.

Cardwell smiled and said, "I thought you might."

At that same moment, Sean Davis was preparing to spend another night in a cold camp. He was a day's ride from Blue Mesa, although he didn't know it. He had a feeling he knew where Cardwell and Jacks were heading. Cardwell had always talked about this one bank he wanted to hit—said that it might even be his last job. Davis just hoped that the two men wouldn't split up at some point, because then he'd have to choose which trail to follow. He didn't much care about Simon Jacks, who just did whatever Cardwell told him.

The one he wanted to catch up to was Cardwell.

"They're headin' northeast," Ralph Cory said.

"You sound surprised," Thomas said.

"I thought they'd head for Utah Territory."

"And where do you think they're headed now?" James asked.

"Well, it could still be Utah," Cory said, "but it might be Colorado."

"I expected them to split up by now," Rigoberto Colon said.

They were all sitting their horses, waiting for someone—Thomas, most likely—to decide if they should camp or get another half hour under their belts before dark, and now they turned and looked at the Mexican.

"It was just a thought," he said, shrugging. "They must have split the money by now, no?"

"I don't think so," Cory said.

Thomas and James looked at him.

"I think they're waiting to reach a town where they might be able to get some rest, split the money, and plan their next move."

"We've only been tracking them a few days," Thomas said.

"They've been pushing their horses," Cory said, "and so have we."

"And what about the man in the middle?" James asked.

Now the eyes of the other three men landed on him.

"I mean the man between us and them."

"Same thing," Cory said. "We're all pushing our animals, and we either have to rest them or risk having them go lame beneath us."

They'd bypassed several small towns, as the tracks they were following indicated that the other two men had done the same.

"You got a town in mind?" Thomas asked Cory.

"No," Cory said, "just something bigger than the ones we've passed, but not too big, and something strategically situated."

"What is strat—strati—" Colon started.

"He means a town located someplace . . . handy," James explained to him.

"In what way?"

"Well," Cory said, "it would be on the borders of two or three different states, or territories."

"Like Arizona, Utah Territory, and Colorado?" Thomas asked.

"Exactly," Cory said. "If they split up there, they've got their choice of where to go."

"But we can still track them, right?" James asked.

"We can . . ." Cory said.

"Unless?" Thomas asked.

"Unless they switch horses."

"We better keep movin', then," James said.

"Wait," Thomas said. "Ralph is right, the horses need rest."

"And so do we?" Colon offered.

"I can keep ridin'—" James said, but his older brother cut him off.

"No," he said. "We'll camp here, James."

"But—"

"We're still a couple of days behind them,

James," Cory said. "It's not going to do any harm to camp for the night and get a fresh start in the morning."

"But if they stop in a town—"

"Then we'll be able to get some information about them when we reach it," Cory finished. "It's actually the best thing for us if they do stop."

"And split the money?" James asked. "And switch horses?"

"They do all that and they'll attract attention, leaving us a bigger trail to follow," Cory said. "Let's do like your brother says and camp for the night."

All eyes fell on James, who squirmed beneath the attention.

"All right," he said reluctantly. This was all still a learning experience for him. He wanted to absorb all he could from "Ralph Cory."

"Same chores, everyone," Thomas said. He dismounted and handed the reins of his horse to Colon. The others did the same, and the Mexican went off to take care of the horses.

While Cory went to find some wood for a fire, James said to Thomas, "Do you trust him?"

"Cory?" Thomas asked. "Or Berto?"

"Well . . . both of 'em."

"Pa trusted them enough to send them along with us," Thomas said, clapping his brother on the back. "That's good enough for me."

41

"We're takin' a chance checkin' into a hotel," Simon Jacks told Cardwell.

"What's life without takin' a few risks, Jacks?" Cardwell asked. "Besides, we need a room so we can finally count the money, and split it up."

"Well, I'm for that."

They got one room with two beds, and carried their saddlebags upstairs. Blue Mesa was not a big town, but it had two hotels and a few saloons, and that was big enough. There would be enough activity for the two of them to go unnoticed, but for now they had business to conduct behind closed doors.

Cardwell was the first to upend his saddlebags and empty the money onto the bed, but Jacks was right behind him. Before long the bed was covered with money.

"I told you that bank was worth hittin'," Cardwell said.

"Yeah, you did," Jacks said, "and you didn't lie."

"Well," Cardwell said, getting on his knees next to the bed, "let's start countin'."

Sean Davis had no choice but to make cold camps along the way because all he had in his saddlebags was some beef jerky. He chewed on the last of it while he wondered if there was a posse behind him, and, if there was, whether they were looking for Cardwell and Jacks, or also looking for him. When it came right down to it, he hadn't done anything wrong. He'd been holding the horses when the shooting started, and nobody could place him in the bank. If there was a posse and they caught up to him, they couldn't touch him. If they tried, then he'd just give them Cardwell and Jacks.

Davis was unaware that Cardwell and Jacks had killed everyone in the bank, but he did know that they'd left him and the others behind to be killed while they got away with all the money.

Davis also knew that Cardwell and Jacks had been making camp each night and eating well, because he'd made sure both horses had supplies on them. But there was only a few days' worth, so they would need to stop in a town soon, not only to divvy up the money, but to outfit themselves.

It was funny. He knew that Cardwell and Jacks didn't respect him, but they were the ones who needed more than just beef jerky and water to survive. Cardwell had insisted that he be sure to include coffee and beans among the supplies. Davis knew he could last a long time on some jerky and a canteen of water, which was why he'd been able to close the gap between himself and them. If they did stop in a town, he'd catch up to them by midday.

If there was a posse, though, he wondered if they were as far behind him as he was behind Cardwell and Jacks.

James handed Thomas a plate of beans and a cup of coffee, then sat back to eat his own meal. Cory and Colon were also seated around the fire, as the four men had taken to having their meals altogether. It was safer that way, and they were getting to know each other a little better.

While they all now knew who Ralph Cory really was, nothing had yet been said about Rigoberto Colon. Though the Mexican always seemed to be in good humor, he was never very forthcoming with information about his past.

"So who has any idea how much money was taken out of the bank?" Cory asked.

"None of us do," Thomas said. "We weren't around long enough after the robbery to find that out."

"All we know is that they killed everyone in the bank and got away with some money," James said.

Cory shook his head. "I wonder if the amount of money they got was worth the number of people they killed."

"How could it be?" James asked. "There isn't enough money—"

"I meant to them, James," Cory said. "These men are not like us. They think differently, have different values. All they care about is money, and they don't care how many people they have to kill to get it."

"Which I guess," Thomas said, "answers your original question."

Cory looked at him. "Yeah."

James found a stream, and not only took the plates there to wash them, but carried everyone's canteen to refill. Colon went to check on the horses, leaving Thomas and Cory alone at the fire.

"How well did James know the girl?" Cory asked. "The mayor's daughter."

"He didn't know her at all," Thomas said. "Not really. He was sweet on her, opened an account at the bank so he could go in and see her whenever he wanted to, but he never really got up the nerve to talk to her."

"I guess that doesn't keep him from being . . . upset over her death," Cory said.

"No," Thomas said, "it doesn't."

"Thomas, tell me about what happened last year," Cory said then. "I've heard some stories, but . . ."

"My mother was killed," Thomas said, "ridden down by bank robbers who had hit the Bank of

Epitaph, Texas. It was the Langer gang. We tracked them down, killed most of them, and sent Ethan Langer to prison."

"I heard he was . . . crippled."

"I did that," Thomas said. "I'm not proud of it. Might have been better if I'd killed him, but I wanted him to suffer." He paused, then added, "He'd just killed my brother Matthew."

"I'm sorry," Cory said. "It must have been hard, losing your mother and your brother."

"To the same man," Thomas said. "Sometimes I think . . ."

Cory waited, and when Thomas didn't continue, he said, "Think what?"

"Sometimes I wonder . . . if my pa doesn't hate me because I didn't kill Ethan. Or because I didn't give him the chance to do it."

"Did you ever talk to him about it?"

"No," Thomas said. "None of the three of us . . . we don't talk about that time very much."

"Maybe you should," Cory said.

"Yeah," Thomas said, "maybe."

At that moment James returned from the stream, and then Colon came over and announced that the horses were fine.

"Time to turn in," Thomas said. "Same watches okay?"

The other three men nodded. They'd been keeping watch in the same order since the first night on the trail.

Thomas wrapped himself in his blanket and put his head on his saddle, thinking over his conversation with Ralph Cory. He'd already discussed the events of the previous year more with him than he ever had with his father. Maybe that was something he should fix when he and James got back to Vengeance Creek.

42

In the morning, Ben Cardwell woke first. Simon Jacks, in the next bed, snored noisily. Under Jacks's arm were his saddlebags, which now contained close to ten thousand dollars, the same amount that was in Cardwell's saddlebags.

Cardwell sat up and swung his feet to the floor. He was disappointed by the amount of money the saddlebags had yielded. Spread on the bed before they'd counted it, it had seemed like more, but many of the bills were of small denomination. Jacks was satisfied with his take, so much so that he'd taken his money to bed with him. But Cardwell wanted more, and he knew where to get it: the one bank he had not yet tried to rob. But in order to get it done, he was going to need Jacks, and a few more men.

Of course, if word got out about what had happened in Vengeance Creek, he'd never get the men he needed to follow him. All the more reason he needed Simon Jacks, and that meant keeping the man happy.

He stood up, dressed quietly, stuck his saddlebags underneath the bed, then left the room to go downstairs and have some breakfast alone. He needed to do some thinking.

Davis stumbled from his bedroll early, had his last mouthful of jerky, and washed it down with water from his canteen. He knew the area, and knew that he wasn't far from Blue Mesa. That might even have been the town Cardwell and Jacks had stopped in. If not, he could at least get some supplies there and continue to follow their trail—even though he had the feeling that he knew where it would lead.

Thomas made a fresh pot of coffee and then woke the other four.

"I'll get breakfast going," James said as he tossed back his blanket and got to his feet.

"Let's make do with coffee this mornin', James," Thomas said. "I want to get an early start."

James looked at Cory and Colon, who were staggering to their feet sleepily.

"Suits me," Cory said. "Quicker we get this all done, the quicker I get back to my shop."

"Berto?" Thomas said.

"We can always eat," Colon said.

"Coffee, then," James said.

"I already made a pot."

James looked at Thomas and said, "Oh, your coffee?"

"What's the matter with my coffee?"

"I'll let them decide if we should drink yours," James said, "or if I should make a new pot."

"Make a new pot," Cory said, "please."

Thomas looked at Colon. "Berto?"

"Sorry, Tomas," Colon said. "I agree."

"Fine," Thomas said, "go ahead."

"Don't be mad, big brother," James said, patting Thomas on the back. "Good coffee is an art."

"An art?" Thomas said as his brother went to the fire. "How much of an art can it be to toss a handful of coffee into some hot water?"

"Well," James said, picking up the existing pot of coffee, "for one thing, you've got to wait for the water to boil."

"You don't wait for the coffee to boil?" Cory asked.

"It'll boil eventually," Thomas said defensively.

James shook his head, upended the pot and poured out his brother's coffee. He then reached for a canteen.

"Watch and learn, big brother," he said, placing the pot on the fire.

Before they broke camp it was Thomas's job to go to the stream and refill the canteens while the others enjoyed James's coffee. He was crouching over the water, filling the last canteen, when he heard a footfall behind him. He dropped the canteen and turned, reaching for his gun.

"I wouldn't," a man's voice said.

Thomas stopped his hand but completed the turn. The man was older than him, but younger than Ralph Cory, probably around thirty-five or so. And he was holding a rifle on him.

"That's a unfriendly move," the man said.

"So's sneakin' up on someone."

"I wasn't sneakin'," the man said. "If I was, you never would've heard me."

"Still," Thomas said, "you're the one holdin' the rifle."

"So I am," the man said. "Tell me, is that coffee I smell?"

"Yes."

"Well, I won't kill you if you'll invite me for a cup," the man said. "How's that sound?"

"Consider yourself invited."

Abruptly, the man raised his rifle barrel and said, "Finish refilling your canteens, then."

Thomas did so and stood up. "Camp is this way."

The man fell into step with him and said, "My name is Forbes, Hal Forbes."

"Thomas Shaye."

"Deputy, I see."

"Yes."

"Tell me," Forbes said, as they walked toward the camp, "is the coffee good?"

"That's what my brother tells me."

At the camp, Thomas made the introductions and gave Forbes the cup of coffee he'd promised for not killing him.

"It's a good thing you're not havin' a cup of Thomas's coffee," James said after hearing the promise. "You'd have killed him anyway."

They all had a laugh at the expense of Thomas's coffee, and he made a silent promise not to ever make another pot of coffee again, no matter who begged him.

"You don't mind me sayin' so," Forbes commented, "you fellas sort of look like a posse."

"We are," Thomas said. "James and I are deputies out of Vengeance Creek. Ralph and Rigoberto are—well, they were pressed into service, I guess you'd say."

"Vengeance Creek?" Forbes said with a frown. "That's quite a ways south. You trackin' your men north?"

"We are."

"Any farther north and you'll be out of Arizona," he said. "Your badges won't be much good then. How far you boys willin' to go?"

"As far as it takes," James said. "The men we're after robbed a bank and killed a lot of people."

"A lot?" Forbes asked.

"Everyone who worked in it," Thomas said. "They executed them."

"And you intend to catch them and execute them?" Forbes asked.

"Maybe—" James started, but he was cut off by Thomas.

"We intend to catch them and bring them back to be tried in court," he said. "That's our job."

Forbes looked at each of them in turn, then said, "I see."

"Tell me, Mr. Forbes," Ralph Cory said, "what brings you out here?"

"Me?" Forbes asked. "I work here."

"Here?" James asked.

"You're on the Double W land."

"Double W?" Thomas asked.

"It's a ranch—"

"I know what it is. Who owns it?"

"A man named William Wilson," Forbes said. "I work for him. I'm the foreman."

"What are you doin' out here?" James asked. "Isn't a foreman supposed to supervise his men?"

"I'm out checking for strays."

"Horse?" Thomas asked.

"Cattle?" Cory asked.

"Both," Forbes said, "and men." He finished his coffee, dumped the dregs on the fire, and stood up. "Thanks for the coffee."

"Mr. Forbes—" Thomas said.

"Call me Hal."

"Hal," Thomas said, "the men we're chasing rode into Vengeance Creek on Double W horses."

Forbes frowned. "What were their names?"

"Ben Cardwell and Sean Davis."

"These the two you're chasin'?"

"Them and one other," Thomas said. "We're not sure of his name, but two of them are definitely Cardwell and Davis. Do those names ring a bell?"

"Can't say that they do."

"What about your boss?" Thomas asked. "Would he know them?"

"I guess you'd have to ask him that."

"We can't stop to do that, Thomas," James said. "The trail will grow cold."

Thomas was in a quandary. He thought that William Wilson would be worth talking to, but did he do it himself and allow James to continue to follow the trail? Or should he send James to the ranch to talk with the man and continue on himself?

"James," he said, "it's worth talking to Mr. Wilson about."

"Send Colon."

"That's not why he's here."

"Then Cory."

"Same reason."

"Why me?"

"I didn't say you."

"But you were gonna."

"I gotta get back," Forbes said. "I saw your fire, smelled it, figured I'd check it out. Since you're lawmen, I got no beef with you. I gotta get back to work. Is somebody comin' with me?"

"Yes," Thomas said, "I am."

"Thomas—"

"Just keep following the trail, James," Thomas said. "I'll be able to follow the one left by you and Ralph and Berto."

"Take Berto with you," James suggested.

"No reason to," Thomas said. "I'm just gonna talk to Mr. Wilson, see if he knows either of the men who were ridin' his horses. I'll be along in no time." He turned to Forbes. "Just let me get my horse and I'll be right with you."

"Sure," Forbes said. "Left my horse back a ways. We can pick him up and ride back to the ranch."

"Fine." Thomas turned and exchanged a glance with Cory, who followed him to the horses.

"You want me to watch James?" he asked.

"I'd be obliged," Thomas said.

"You're doing the right thing, Thomas," Cory said. "Berto and I can take care of him."

"Yeah, well," Thomas said, saddling his horse, "don't let him know you're takin' care of him, understand?"

"Perfectly."

"He's still the one with the badge."

"I know it," Cory said. "Berto and I are just . . . volunteers, sort of."

"This shouldn't put me more than half a day behind you," Thomas said, turning his horse so he could mount up.

"Maybe, like your brother said, you should take Rigoberto along to watch your back," Cory said.

"Against what?" Thomas asked. "I'm just gonna ask the man some questions." He mounted up. "I'll be fine."

"You better be," Cory said. "I don't want to have to explain to your father that I let you go off alone."

"You didn't let me do anythin'," Thomas said. "My decision, remember?"

"I remember."

"I'll see you soon."

Thomas rode back to where Forbes was waiting, extended a hand and pulled the man up behind him.

"See you, little brother," he said. "Keep on the trail. I'll catch up soon."

"Be careful," James said.

"Keep these other two in line."

"Count on it."

As Cory reached the fire, Thomas rode off, following Forbes's directions to his horse.

"I think one of you should have gone with him," James said to Cory and Colon.

"His decision, James," Cory said.

"Yeah, well," James said, "I'm wearin' a badge, and I get to make some decisions too . . . don't I?"

44

Thomas found Hal Forbes's horse and then waited while the man mounted up. It may not have been absolutely necessary for him to go to the Double W ranch, but if there was even a chance he might find out something to help them get ahead of robbers, he wanted to take it.

"We're not that far from the house," Forbes said. "Just ride along with me."

They rode side by side, and in the course of asking questions, Forbes heard Thomas's full name. "Shaye?" he said.

"That's right."

"As in Sheriff Dan Shaye of Vengeance Creek?"

"Right again."

"I heard about you and your father," Forbes said. "You tracked down the Langer gang."

"More people have heard about that than I thought," Thomas said.

"Well, that was something for you and your pa and your brothers to do."

"It wasn't such a somethin'," Thomas said.

"Well, Mr. Wilson's gonna be glad to meet you."

"Why's that?"

"He likes meetin' men with reputations."

"I don't have a reputation."

"You outdrew Ethan Langer," Forbes said, "and then you didn't kill him. You crippled him and sent him to prison."

"I know what I did, Mr. Forbes."

"It's Hal."

"Hal," Thomas said, "I ain't proud of what I done to Ethan Langer. More and more I think I shoulda just killed him."

"What you did was worse," Forbes said, with undisguised admiration, "much worse."

"I know. . . ."

"They're headin' for Colorado," Cory said. "No doubt about that."

"I agree," Colon said.

"Maybe they'll stop someplace first," James offered.

Cory and Colon were on their feet, while James was still mounted and holding the reins of their horses.

"They'll have to," Cory said. "They're going to need supplies."

"That is when they might split up," Colon said,

"and we will have to decide which trail to follow if that happens."

"I know that, Berto," James said. "When that time comes, I'll make the decision."

"*Sí,*" Colon said. "You are *el jefe* now."

The two men mounted up, and the three continued on in silence. James couldn't help but worry about Thomas.

Simon Jacks found Ben Cardwell in the hotel dining room, having breakfast. He had both sets of saddlebags with him when he sat down across from the partner.

"Found yours under the bed," Jacks said. "I couldn't bring myself to leave them in the room, though."

"Just as well," Cardwell said. "We'll have to get movin' right after breakfast."

"Headin' where?" Jacks asked. "You ain't told me where this other bank is yet."

"It's in Colorado."

"But where in Colorado?"

"You'll just have to keep ridin' with me to find out, Simon."

"I'm ready to do that, Ben," Jacks said. "Just let me get a little somethin' into my stomach first."

"Flapjacks are okay," Cardwell said.

Jacks called the waiter over and ordered a tall stack of flapjacks on Cardwell's say so.

* * *

Sean Davis had risen while it was still dark and got an early start. He figured he'd make Blue Mesa by noon. If Cardwell and Jacks were there and they got a late start, he just might catch up to them. If not, then he'd buy a few supplies and just keep going. Davis knew he was the better tracker, and he could see that the trail he was following was growing fresher.

He was getting closer and closer. . . .

"Blue Mesa," Ralph Cory said.

"What's that?" James asked.

"It's a town I know, nestled right in the corner of Arizona, so that you got your choice of where you want to go, Utah Territory or Colorado."

"That's where you think they're goin'?"

"It makes sense." He looked at the Mexican. "What do you think, Berto?"

"*Sí*, Señor Cory," Colon replied, "as you say, it makes sense. I too know of this town. It is not large, but it is the biggest in this part of the country."

"So they'd be able to outfit there," James said.

"They can do whatever they want there," Cory said. "What we have to hope is that they take a rest."

"How long before we make it?"

"If we push," Cory said, "we could get there by nightfall."

James turned in his saddle without stopping his horse and looked behind him.

"He'll be along, James," Cory said. "Thomas will be along."

45

"I didn't notice any packhorses," Forbes said to Thomas as they approached the ranch house. "If you need some, we can probably provide them."

"That's okay. We decided to travel light, hopin' to catch up," Thomas said.

Thomas noticed he was attracting attention from some of the other hands, who stopped what they were doing to watch him and Forbes ride in.

Forbes reined in his horse in front of the house and dismounted, signaling to Thomas to do the same.

"Mr. Wilson will be inside."

"How do you know without checkin'?"

"He never leaves the house." Forbes turned, signaled to one of the watching hands to come over, and handed him his horse's reins. "Give him yours. He'll look after your horse."

"Don't unsaddle him," Thomas said. "I won't be here that long."

"No problem. Come on."

Thomas followed Forbes up the steps to the front door. The house was two stories high with a porch that wrapped around.

"Impressive house."

"Mr. Wilson built it himself."

The foreman opened the front door and led Thomas inside. They were in a large, high-ceilinged living room. The furniture also looked as if someone had made it themselves. Not fancy. But good, solid work.

"Your Mr. Wilson looks like a real do-it-yourself man."

"He was," a woman said.

Thomas turned and found himself looking at a pretty young woman holding a gun on him. When he turned to look at Forbes, he found himself looking down the barrel of a second gun.

"What's goin' on?" he asked.

"That's what you're going to tell us," the woman said.

"Whataya say, Doc?" Dan Shaye asked.

Doc Simpson looked at him, wiping his hands dry on a towel. "What are you asking me?"

"Can I sit a horse?"

"You want that wound to open and start bleeding again, yeah, sure," the sawbones said. "You thinking of doing that?"

"That's just what I was thinkin' of doin," Shaye said. He slipped off the doctor's table and started buttoning his shirt. "It's been a week, and I need to go after them."

"Sheriff," Simpson said, "you got lucky with that bullet, but if that wound gets infected—"

"You got it wrapped nice and tight, Doc," Shaye said. "What else would I have to do?"

Simpson stared at him for a few moments, then shrugged.

"Keep it clean," he said. "If it starts to bleed, clean it out with some whiskey, wrap it again. Just don't let it fester and get infected."

"How will I know if it's infected?"

"Don't worry," Simpson said. "You'll smell it."

"Thanks, Doc."

"Don't thank me," the doctor said. "Just don't come back dead."

Shaye went to see the mayor, who was sitting in his office with a half empty bottle of whiskey in his hand.

"That's not helpin'."

"She's dead," Timmerman said. "Nothing's going to bring her back."

"Now you feel guilty?" Shaye asked. "A week later."

Timmerman took a drink from the bottle, wiped his mouth on the back of his hand and asked, "What do you want, Sheriff?"

"I'm goin' after them myself," Shaye said.

"Your boys are probably dead too."

"I don't think so," Shaye said, "but thanks for

the thought." He walked to the door. "I'll find someone to deputize in my stead."

"I don't care," Timmerman said.

"You will," Shaye said, "once that bottle's empty. I'm gonna bring the money back, Mayor, and the bank robbers."

Timmerman waved a hand, but Shaye was gone.

At the livery, he saddled his horse and tied a canvas bag to the saddle horn. All he needed was some beef jerky, some coffee, and a canteen. He was going to travel fast.

"You and your boys comin' back, Sheriff?" Ron Hill asked.

"We'll be back, Hill," Shaye said. "Meanwhile . . ." He took a deputy's badge from his pocket and pinned it on the liveryman's chest. ". . . you're in charge."

"What?" he said as Shaye mounted up. "I'm no lawman."

"That's okay," Shaye said. "The mayor's no mayor either. Just keep the office clean."

He rode out of the livery, leaving Hill to sputter his protests behind him. All he was concerned with was getting his boys back, along with the money and the bank robbers. After that he had a feeling they'd be leaving Vengeance Creek as far behind them as they'd hoped to leave Epitaph.

46

"I don't understand," Thomas said. "I only came here to ask some questions."

"Hal?"

"He and some others were down by the stream," Forbes replied. "Said they were trackin' some men who were ridin' some of our horses. Said they were law."

"Deputies," Thomas said, indicating the badge on his chest, "from Vengeance Creek."

"You're a little far from home." She was a woman, but just barely, probably twenty-four or -five. She was wearing a man's work shirt and jeans, and a pair of work-worn boots.

"Who are you?" Thomas asked.

"My name's Wendy Wilson."

"I came here to talk to your—"

"Father," she said. "My father."

"Is he here?"

"He's dead," she said. "He was killed about

two weeks ago. The men who killed him stole some horses."

"Okay, I think I understand," Thomas said. "The men I'm trackin' are also the men who killed your father. They came to Vengeance Creek and hit our bank, killed all the people who worked in it."

"Hal?" the pretty girl said.

"I believe him, Wendy."

"If you'll put your guns down," Thomas said, "we can talk about it."

"There's not much to talk about," Wendy Wilson said, "but we'll put our guns down."

She lowered hers, followed by Hal Forbes.

"Sorry," Forbes said, "but we can't be too careful."

Thomas thought the man might have had cause to be suspicious, but that he also might have produced his gun to impress the woman—because she was his boss now, or for some other reason?

"Do you know the names of the men who killed your father?" Thomas asked Wendy.

She went to a chair and sat down. The gun dangled between her legs, forgotten. Forbes had holstered his. Now he walked to the girl and took the gun from her. She hardly noticed.

"We don't know their names," she said.

"We never did," Forbes said.

"What happened?"

"They rode up on us while the hands were out," Wendy said. "We offered them refreshments,

which they took . . . and then they took more."
She turned her face away.

"They killed Mr. Wilson, raped Wendy, and took some horses," Forbes finished.

"I'm sorry . . . What about the law?"

"Local law ain't worth much," Forbes said. "I tracked them for a while, but lost them. I ain't no bounty hunter. None of us are. We had to give up."

"So there's nothin' you can tell me about them?"

"You want to know what they look like," Wendy asked, "down there?"

"Uh . . . no," Thomas said. "No, I don't." He turned to Forbes, because looking at Wendy Williams made him uncomfortable. "I better catch up to the rest of my party."

"Sure," Forbes said.

"I'm not at all sure why you let me come here, Mr. Forbes."

"To tell you the truth, Deputy," Forbes said, "neither am I."

Thomas turned to the woman again. "Ma'am, we're gonna catch these men. I promise you that."

"My father's dead," she said. "Catching them won't bring him back."

"But . . . for what they did to you . . ."

She stood up abruptly and glared at him. "I'll live, Deputy," she said. "It was just sex, wasn't it?"

Before Thomas could answer, she turned and walked out of the room, leaving an awkward silence behind.

"I, uh, guess I'll be goin'."

Forbes nodded and walked him out. He had Thomas's horse brought up to the front of the house.

"I can let you have some men, if you like," Forbes said. "Ranch hands, not gun hands."

"That's all right," Thomas said, mounting up. "I think we'll be able to handle it."

Thomas rode off the Double W property with only a couple of answers to his questions. One, they knew why the two men had ridden into town on Double W horses, and two, he knew exactly what kind of men these were. Killers, yes—but worse. But all in all he hadn't found out anything helpful, and the stop at the Double W ranch only served to put him behind James and the others. Coming here, he decided, had probably been a bad decision.

But not the first, or last, he would ever make.

Jacks looked up as Ben Cardwell came out of the telegraph office.

"Okay," Cardwell said. "The rest of them will be waitin' when we get there."

"The rest of who?" Jacks asked.

"Just some men I know, who I think we can trust to do this job with us."

"We can trust them?"

"Yes."

"But can they trust us?"

"Right up until we get all that money in our

hot little hands," Cardwell said. "Then all bets are off."

"That's what I wanted to hear," Simon Jacks said. "Can we get out of Blue Mesa now? Stupid name for a town."

"Yeah," Cardwell said, "stupid."

As they walked toward the livery, Jacks said, "Now Red Mesa, that'd be a good name for a town. . . ."

47

"Two hours," Ralph Cory said. "No more." He pointed to one particular set of tracks. "These." Then he pointed to the other, original two. "These are older. Yesterday."

"I agree," Colon said.

James was still mounted, twisted around in his saddle so he could look behind them.

Cory and Colon stood and turned to face him.

"Anything?" Cory asked.

"I see some dust . . . I think."

"Berto?" Cory asked.

Colon mounted his horse so he could take advantage of the same vantage point James had.

"Anything?" Cory asked again.

"I see nothing," Colon said.

James looked disappointed. "I thought I saw . . ."

Cory mounted, touched James on the shoulder. "He'll catch up. Don't worry."

"It's just been too soon," James said. "I don't want to lose another brother . . . you know?"

"No," Cory said, "I don't . . . but I think I can imagine."

"It would be better to keep moving," Colon said.

"James?" Cory said.

Reluctantly, James dragged his eyes from the horizon behind them. "Yes," he said. "Okay, let's go."

Thomas was back on the trail, only this time he was tracking his own brother. The trail was fresh, though, and he was moving much faster than they were. He expected to catch up to them in a matter of hours, even if he had to keep riding after they camped, or if they reached the town of Blue Mesa.

Alone with his thoughts during his ride, he couldn't help but wonder about his father. To this day they still had not talked about what had happened between Thomas and Ethan Langer. He knew his father was disappointed that he hadn't killed Langer—rather than crippling him and sending him to prison—and sometimes, when he caught Dan Shaye looking at him, he felt guilty. He'd told his father that he thought killing Ethan Langer would have been too easy, and would have put the man out of his misery. That way, Langer was a cripple, was in prison, and was still haunted in his dreams by Mary Shaye. But either he hadn't done a good job explaining or his father didn't want to listen, or both. Now, if they could talk again, maybe he'd be able to get his father to understand.

Thomas thought he'd been doing too much drinking on the wrong side of town. When this was all over, he was going to try to *make* his father listen to what he had to say. Their relationship was not going to change—for the better—unless they faced what had happened with Ethan Langer and talked about it.

Daniel Shaye was questioning whether upholding the law was something he still wanted to do. It had already cost him a wife and one son. Now he had sent two more sons out wearing badges like targets on their chests. Plus, he himself had been shot two years in a row.

What else was he fit to do? In his entire life he'd been on one side of the law or the other. He was over fifty. Could he settle down someplace and be a storekeeper? A rancher? He didn't know anything about either.

But what about his sons? James was smart— very smart. If he went back to school, Shaye thought he had the makings of a good lawyer. Maybe a doctor. He had potential, he just needed seasoning for it to blossom.

Thomas was different. He had talent with a gun, and he'd already used it to kill men. Shaye saw the raw talent in his oldest son too. Thomas had the potential to be a better gunman and better law-man, he thought, than he himself had ever been.

Shaye shifted in his saddle. His wound was throbbing, but he didn't think it was bleeding. He knew that for the past year he hadn't been a very good father to Thomas. What happened in Oklahoma City with Ethan Langer stuck in his craw. The whole point of the hunt was to find Langer and kill him. What Thomas had done was allow the man to live—crippled, and in prison, but still alive. He had not been able to come to terms with that, but maybe it was time. After this was all over, he told himself, he would talk to both Thomas and James about what had happened and what was going to happen.

All they had to do was all come back from this hunt alive.

48

Sean Davis lost the trail as he entered Blue Mesa. There was just too much traffic on the main street, so the tracks he'd been following were trampled into obscurity. However, he knew if Cardwell and Jacks had stayed in town overnight, they would have put their horses up at the livery stable, of which there was only one.

At the stable, he faced a good news/bad news situation. The good news was that the livery-man—an older man named Hackett—told him he'd just missed Cardwell and Simon Jacks, after a few dollars changed hands.

"Left this mornin'," the man said. "Few hours ago, actually. I knew they looked dodgy. You a lawman?"

Davis didn't answer. He was too busy worrying about the bad news. Of all the places to take a bad step, his horse had done it right in the middle of the main street. The animal almost went down and he had to get off it and walk it to the stable.

"How bad is it?" he asked the liveryman.

"Sprained," the man said. "Not gonna ride this fella for a while."

"I need a horse," Davis said. "You got any for sale?"

"Not me," the older man said, letting the horse's leg drop and brushing his hands off on his pants. "I know where you can get one, but it won't be cheap."

"Where?"

"End of the street you'll see a corral," the man said. "Ask for a man named Ian."

"Ian?"

"Yeah, he's Irish, or Scottish, or somethin'. Foreigner, anyway. Sells horses."

"Okay," Davis said. "Thanks."

"So you ain't a lawman?"

Davis stopped on his way out, turned and said, "No, I ain't a lawman. Take care of my horse and rig for me, I'll be back. Maybe you'll wanna buy the horse?"

"Naw," Hackett said, "I don't buy horses. Better talk to Ian about that too."

"Yeah, okay," Davis said, and left.

"'Nother one on the dodge," Hackett said when he was gone, and began unsaddling the horse.

Davis found that Ian was a Scotsman in his sixties with about half a dozen horses available for sale in his corral. The man had the scarred hands of a longtime horse trader, and Davis knew he was going to get outhaggled no matter what. He could see this was going to take a while, because he recognized that there were no shortcuts with this man.

"I got a jug in the back," Ian said. "We can pass it back and forth while we haggle."

"Get it," Davis said, "and let's get started."

The three riders stopped when they came within sight of Blue Mesa.

"Not a big town," James said.

"We ride in together, word's gonna get around," Ralph Cory said.

"If the men we seek are in town, they will hear," Colon said. "They will be forewarned."

"What do we do, then?" James asked.

The two older men looked at him. James knew what they were thinking. He was the one wearing the badge. He wished Thomas was there.

"Never mind," he said. "Let's ride in separately. I'll go first, then you fellas follow me every fifteen minutes."

"Might help if we ride in from different directions too," Cory suggested.

"Good idea, Ralph," James said.

"Where do we meet?" Colon asked.

"At the livery," James said. "Doesn't look like this town would have more than one, and our horses won't be so obvious there."

"Good thinking," Cory said.

"Thanks," James said, gigging his horse with his heels. "I'll see you boys in town."

"You might want to put that badge in your pocket, though," Cory called after him. "Sun'll glint right off it."

James waved a hand, then removed the badge and tucked it in his shirt pocket.

Entering the livery, James saw an older man rubbing down a horse.

"Help ya?" the man asked.

"I'm lookin' for somebody, might have rode into town a little while ago," James said. "That horse just come in?"

" 'Bout an hour ago," the man said. "Kinda lame, though. Stepped in a hole right here in town."

"Where's the rider?"

"Went lookin' for another horse."

"Where?"

"Far end of town, there's a corral," the man said. "Fella named Ian sells horses."

"Any other strangers in town?"

The man straightened from the horse and looked at James. "You law?"

"Yes."

"Badge?"

James took it out of his pocket and showed it to the man, but didn't hold it close enough for him to read it.

"Two others, left this mornin'," he said. "This third fella seems to be trailin' them, like you. You alone?"

"No."

"Good," the man said. "Y're a might young to be tryin' to take somebody alone."

"I get by," James said.

He was about to say something else when he heard a noise behind him. He turned quickly and saw Colon entering the livery on foot, leading his horse.

"He with you?" the liveryman asked.

"Yes."

"Well," the man said, "you got your choice. Ian's gonna keep yer man hagglin' for a while, probably over a jug. You can take 'im there, or here when he comes back for his rig."

Colon eyed James.

"Our man's lookin' for a new horse," James explained. "Two other men rode out earlier this mornin'."

"Which way?" Colon asked.

James looked at the liveryman.

"I dunno," the man said. "I didn't watch them leave."

"Describe them," James said, and listened while the man did.

"That them?" Colon asked.

"One of 'em sounds like Cardwell," James said. "We'll wait for Cory, and then go down and take the one in town while he's hagglin' over a jug with the horse trader."

"As you wish, *Jefe*," Colon said. "You are in charge."

"He's the boss?" the liveryman asked, surprised.

"You got a problem with that?" James asked.

"Me? I got no problems. Uh, am I gonna get paid for takin' care of this fella's horse?"

"You'll get paid," James said. "Just don't leave here until we get back."

"I ain't goin' nowhere," the man said.

James jerked his head at Colon, and they walked their horses outside to wait for Cory.

49

"Then we have a deal?" Ian asked Davis.

"You drive a hard bargain," Davis said, knowing this was what the man wanted to hear. "Yeah, we got a deal."

"I'll jus' need to take a look at your horse, laddie," Ian said.

"It's a sound animal," Davis promised, "other than the sprain."

"Why don't we walk over and take a look?"

"Fine with me."

"One more pull from the jug, though, lad," Ian said, handing it over to Davis.

"One more," Davis agreed, even though the homegrown squeezin' had already burnt the roof of his mouth, as well as his throat. He had to admit, though, that the fire it stoked in his belly was well worth it. He took a healthy pull and handed it back. Ian took a swig that was twice as long, then wiped his mouth with the back of his hand.

"Be warned, lad," Ian said, "stand up slow and easy. This stuff will knock you right off yer feet."

"I can handle it—" Davis said, but as he stood up he suddenly got dizzy and fell back into his chair.

"Told you," Ian said, laughing.

James, Cory, and Colon decided to leave their horses at the livery and walk over to the horse trader's corral. Behind the corral was a shack, where they assumed the haggling was going on. As they approached it, they heard somebody laughing from inside.

"How do you want to play this, James?" Cory asked.

"Seems to me," James said, "the best way would be to wait for him to come out. Goin' in might spook him, and we want to take him alive. He might know where the others are headed."

"Okay," Cory said. "Looks like there's only one way in, so let's cover it."

Davis waited for the room to stop spinning before he tried to stand up again. This time he remained on his feet.

"You okay?" Ian asked.

"What's in that stuff?" Davis asked.

"That's a family secret, lad," Ian said. "Let's go over to the livery and take a look at your horse."

"After you," Davis said.

Ian stepped out of the shack and was immediately grabbed from one side. James shook his head, indicating that it wasn't the man they were looking for, and he was simply yanked to one side by Colon, who held his finger to his lips. Ian, who wanted no trouble, put his hands in the air and shrugged.

Davis came through the door next and immediately saw James, who had put his badge back on. He reached for his gun, but stopped short when he felt a gun barrel pressed to his temple.

"I wouldn't," Ralph Cory said.

Davis didn't move as Cory plucked the gun from his holster and tucked it into Cory's belt.

"Step outside," James said, "slowly."

Davis came out, lifted his hands in the air.

"I didn't do nothin','" he said. "Who are you guys?"

"I'm a deputy from Vengeance Creek," James said. "You're under arrest for robbing the Vengeance Creek bank and killin' everyone inside."

"I didn't kill nobody."

"You were part of the gang that did."

"You can't prove that," Davis said.

"We'll prove it," James said. "You can help yourself by tellin' us where those other two are headed."

"What other two?"

"Okay," James said, "play it that way. Berto, bring that other one around."

The Mexican stepped back and allowed Ian to come from the side of the shack.

"What's your name?" James asked.

"Ian McShane," the man said. "I am a horse trader, just met this lad today."

"You got law in this town?"

"Sheriff Gibney," Ian said.

"Any deputies?"

"One."

James looked at Colon and Cory.

"Let's take him over to the local lockup," he suggested. "We can talk to him more there."

"You can't put me in jail," Davis insisted. "I ain't done nothin'."

"You've done plenty," Cory said, "and we all know it. What's your name, anyway? Any paper out on you?"

Davis kept quiet.

"Told me his name was Davis," Ian offered.

"Let's go, Davis," James said.

Cory prodded Davis in the back with his gun and they started walking toward the sheriff's office.

"Guess he's not going to be buyin' a horse from me," Ian said.

"Maybe not," James said, "but we might. We'll need one to get him out of town."

"Got just the one for you," Ian said happily. "We can haggle over a jug."

"Maybe later," James said, and followed after the others.

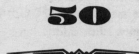

50

Sheriff Jarrod Gibney looked up as his office door burst open and four men came tumbling through.

"What the hell—"

"Deputy James Shaye, Sheriff," James said, introducing himself. "From Vengeance Creek, Arizona."

"Arizona?" Gibney asked. "Deputy, you're a little out of your bailiwick, ain't ya?"

"That may be," James said, "but I got a prisoner for you."

"That's so?" The sheriff stood up, showing that his belly had popped a button at the bottom of his shirt. There was also something on his bushy mustache, maybe left over from breakfast. "What'd he do?"

"He's part of a gang that robbed our bank and killed everyone who worked in it."

"Everyone?"

"Every last employee," James said.

"I ain't killed nobody."

"Might be some paper on this one, Sheriff," Cory said.

"These fellas also deputies?" Gibney asked.

"Posse," James said. "This here's Ralph Cory, that's Rigoberto Colon."

"Three man posse?"

"Four," James said. "My brother's comin' up behind us. He's also a deputy."

"I haven't heard nothin' about this Vengeance Creek bank job you're talkin about—" the sheriff started, but James cut him off.

"Can we talk about it after we put him in a cell, Sheriff?"

"Huh? Oh, sure. Follow me."

They went into a back room, where there was only one cell. Cory and Colon remained in the office, while James and Gibney put Davis inside the cell.

"We're still trackin' two men, Sheriff," James said. "We'd like to leave Davis here so we can get on with it."

"Well . . . for how long?"

"Until we come back."

"And what do I do if you don't come back?"

"Contact Sheriff Dan Shaye in Vengeance Creek," Cory said. "He'll arrange to have the prisoner picked up."

Gibney looked at Cory. "Do I know you?" he asked.

"I don't think so."

"You look real familiar to me."

"I get that a lot," Cory said. "I've got that kind of face."

"Sheriff," James said, "my brother should be along shortly. His name's Thomas Shaye. If you'd tell him what happened here and that we continued on our way, I'd be much obliged."

Now Gibney looked at James. "You're awful young to be a deputy, ain't ya?"

"I'm old enough," James said. "Will you give my brother that message?"

"Well, yeah, but . . . I don't know about keepin' this feller here for too long—"

"I'm gonna talk with him before we leave," James said, "see what he can tell me about the others we're chasin'." He turned to Colon and Cory. "Why don't you fellas meet me in the saloon?"

Cory, relieved not to have to remain in the office with a lawman who might have recognized him from his bounty hunting days, said, "That suits me."

"*Sí,* me also," Colon said.

"We'll see you later," Cory said, and the two men left the office.

"That Cory feller sure looks familiar," Gibney said.

"I'm gonna talk with the prisoner," James said. "Would you sit in so you can tell my brother what's been said?" He figured this would also keep the man from dwelling too long on where he'd seen "Ralph Cory" before.

"Sure, okay," Gibney said, and they went into the single cell block.

51

"Where do you think he knows you from?" Colon asked Cory when they were in the saloon.

"I don't know," Cory said. "Someplace in my past. I probably brought him a prisoner once."

"Or a body," Colon said.

Cory ignored him.

"Do you recognize him?" the Mexican asked.

"No," Cory said. "I got too much to do rememberin' the faces of the men I killed. I can't be rememberin' the faces of all the lawmen I've known over the years."

"*Sí,*" Colon said, "that makes sense."

"It don't matter," Cory said. "We'll be leavin' this town soon."

"Too bad we do not have time for a hot meal," Colon said.

Cory looked at him and asked, "Who says we don't?"

They both smiled, and Cory started waving frantically to the bartender.

"You serve food here?" he asked.

"It'll go easier on you if you cooperate, Davis," James said to Sean Davis.

The man was laying on his back on the cot in his cell, one arm thrown across his eyes, ignoring him.

"They left you behind to take the rap, didn't they?"

No answer.

"Took off with your share of the money."

Silence.

"This guy's an idiot," Gibney said. "Those others did that to him and he's protectin' them?"

"I ain't protectin' nobody," Davis finally said, without moving his arm.

"Then why won't you talk to me?" James asked.

Davis fell back into his silence.

"Oh, I get it," James said.

"What?" Gibney asked.

James turned to face the lawman. "He was trackin' them too," he said. "He wants to find them as much as we do."

"Do we know who any of these fellas are?"

"Yeah," James said. "One of them is named Ben Cardwell. The other one might be a man named Simon Jacks."

"Jacks?"

"Yeah," James said. "You know him?"

"I know of him."

"Like what?"

"Good man with a gun," the lawman said, "good man to hire."

"Not a leader?"

"No," Gibney said. "From what I've heard, he is strictly for hire. Somebody else does the thinkin'."

"Like this fella Cardwell," James said.

"Probably."

They both looked into the cell again.

"I don't believe this one does any thinkin'," James said. "He looks like a definite follower."

"Yeah," Gibney said. "I don't even know why he was trackin' them. A man like Simon Jacks would kill him with no problem."

Davis removed his arm from his eyes so he could look at them, then turned and faced the wall. James signaled for the sheriff to follow him out.

"It doesn't look like I'm gonna get anythin' from him," he said in the office. "I'd better just collect my men and get after the other two."

"Whatever you say, Deputy."

"My brother will be along later today," James said. "Just tell him what happened and where we went."

"All right," Gibney said. But as James was going out the door, he called out, "But where *are* you going?"

* * *

James found Cory and Colon at the saloon, each with a beer and hot plate of food in front of them.

"I see you fellas haven't missed me," he said.

"Bartender, bring out that other plate!" Cory said, then looked at James. "We thought there was no harm in havin' some hot food before we left."

The bartender obeyed, bringing out a third plate of food, along with a mug of beer. James sat down in front of the beer and looked around. The saloon was empty but for them. It was early, but it wasn't that early.

"Where's everyone else?" he asked.

"I think they thought there was gonna be trouble," Cory said.

James hesitated with a forkful of steak halfway to his mouth. "Do you think there are others here?"

"No, I think the other two left, and the only reason we caught Davis is that his horse went lame. Did you get anything out of him?"

"No, nothing." James took a bite of steak. It was tough, but good.

"Do you want me to try?" Cory asked.

"No," James said, "Thomas will be along soon. He'll have a try. We should eat and get going."

"We need some supplies," Colon said.

"That'll be your job, Berto," James said. "Just get us some beef jerky and coffee."

"No bacon? No *frijoles*?"

"No," James said. "We want to outfit light and move fast."

"Sounds good," Cory said.

"*Sí*," Colon said, "as you wish, *Jefe*."

Cory looked at James. The young man thought the older man might have winked at him, but it could have been his imagination.

52

When Thomas rode into Blue Mesa, the main street was empty. He found that odd. Perhaps something had happened in town that sent everyone indoors. Or the threat of something. He preferred if the answer were the latter, not the former.

There were a couple of ways he could have played this, but he decided to go at it in a straightforward manner. If something had happened, the local sheriff would know it.

He continued to ride until he saw the sheriff's office, then reined his horse in right in front. He dismounted, tied off his horse, approached the door, then stopped to turn and survey the street. He had the feeling he was being watched from windows. He wondered if any of those people were holding a gun on him.

He turned and entered the office. A portly man with a big mustache was seated behind the desk.

"Sheriff?"

"That's right," the man said. "Sheriff Gibney . . . and you must be Deputy Shaye."

"That's right, Thomas Shaye. I assume my brother was here?"

"He was," Gibney said, "he and his two men."

"Are they all right?"

"They're fine," Gibney said. "They had a hot meal and went on their way, but they left somethin' behind."

"What's that?"

Gibney waved his hand and said, "In my cell."

Thomas followed, saw a man still lying with his back to the outside of the cell.

"Who is it?'

"A man named Davis," Gibney said. "Your brother seemed to think he was part of the gang that robbed your bank."

Thomas looked at Gibney. "Tell me about it. . . ."

After the lawman had told him everything he knew, Thomas asked him to open the cell door.

"And then what?"

"And then leave me alone with him," Thomas said. "I'm gonna ask him some questions."

"Your brother tried that."

"I'm gonna ask a little more forcefully."

Davis turned over and looked at Thomas as he came through the open cell door. . . .

* * *

Ben Cardwell and Simon Jacks crossed into Colorado.

"You want to tell me where we're headed?" Jacks asked. "Where this special bank is?"

"You'll find out," Cardwell said. "Just know that there's a lot of money ahead of us, Jacks. More than you could imagine."

"That's ahead of us," Jacks said. "What do you think is behind us?"

"What does it matter?" Cardwell asked. "Davis, a posse. By the time they catch up to us, we'll have a dozen guns behind us. We'll take care of them, and then my bank."

"Your bank?"

Cardwell looked at Jacks. "Our bank, Simon. Our bank."

"The trail is clear from here," Ralph Cory said.

James and Colon had remained mounted. The Mexican had long since admitted that the ex-bounty hunter was a better tracker than he was. He was there mostly for his gun, when trouble came.

It had taken them some time to relocate the trail, but once they were far enough from town that the ground wasn't filled with tracks from town traffic, Cory had picked it up again.

Cory turned and mounted up, accepted the reins of his horse from James.

"They're still together," he said. "Still heading northeast."

"Colorado," Colon said.

"Looks like it." He looked at James. "We gonna follow them all the way?"

James nodded. "All the way."

"You remember who I am?" Thomas asked Sean Davis.

The man sat up on his cot and stared at Thomas without answering.

"I'm the deputy who's gonna beat you to death if you don't start talkin'," Thomas said to him.

Davis stared at the badge on Thomas's chest, then looked past him.

"W-Where's the sheriff?" he asked.

"He left," Thomas said. "Went for a walk. I told him to leave us alone so we could . . . talk."

"I—I got nothin' to say to you."

"Yeah," Thomas said, "yeah, you do, friend . . . you just don't know it yet."

He took out his knife and moved closer. "I need to know what you know, Davis, but if you won't tell me, then I don't see that you have any need of your tongue . . . do you?"

Davis blinked at him and said, "Huh?"

"Let me make it simple," Thomas explained. "If you don't talk to me, I'm gonna cut out your tongue."

"You—You can't do that."

"Sure I can."

"Y-You wouldn't."

"Yes," Thomas said, "I would."

"B-But—"

"You ever hear of Ethan Langer?"

Davis's eyes popped and he skittered back on his cot until the wall stopped him. "That was you?"

"Now let me ask my questions again. . . ."

53

When Thomas came out of the sheriff's office, the man was sitting in a wooden chair outside.

"Get what you needed?" Gibney asked.

"Yes."

"You musta been more persuasive than your brother," the sheriff said. "Say, ain't he a little young for this kinda responsibility?"

"He's old enough."

"That's what he said."

"I'm gonna need a fresh mount," Thomas said, "but I don't think I have enough money to buy one. I can trade my mount in, but—"

Gibney stood up. "Let's go and talk to Ian Mc-Shane," he said. "He's the local horse trader. In fact, that's where your brother and them others found your man Davis."

"Is that a fact?"

They started walking down the street, Thomas leading his horse.

"Where's Davis's horse and rig?" he asked the lawman.

"At the livery."

"Maybe I can sweeten the deal by throwin' them in."

"Could be."

They walked a few moments and then Gibney asked, "That feller Cory, ridin' with your brother?"

"What about him?"

"He sure looked familiar to me," the lawman said. "Where'd he come from?"

"He's just a local, from Vengeance Creek," Thomas said. "He volunteered."

"And the Mex?"

"Also a volunteer."

"Well, I don't know him," Gibney said, "but I'm sure I know Cory from someplace. It'll come to me."

Thomas hoped not.

When they reached the corral and shack at the end of town, Gibney stopped Thomas.

"Ian's a fierce haggler," he explained. "You won't be able to buy a horse from him without it."

"Okay."

"And how are you on squeezin's?"

"What?"

"Never mind," Gibney said, patting Thomas on the arm, "just follow my lead, and maybe you'll come out of it with a fresh horse and just a little bit of a headache."

* * *

Sweetening the deal with Sean Davis's horse and outfit had done the job for him. Thomas also promised to send Ian some more money when he returned to Vengeance Creek. With Sheriff Gibney backing his play, the horse trader had finally agreed.

He was tightening the cinch on his saddle when Gibney walked into the livery.

"Just about ready to go?"

"Almost."

"Sure you don't wanna grab a hot meal?"

"No time."

"You got some idea about where your men are goin'?"

"Davis gave me some idea."

"You believe him?"

"Yeah, I believe him."

Thomas turned his new horse, a five-year-old bay mare Ian swore had the stamina of a bull, and walked her out of the livery. Thomas usually rode colts, or geldings, but the trader swore this was the best horse he had. Though he was not as good a judge of horseflesh as his father and younger brother, from what he could see, the man was telling the truth.

The sheriff followed him out of the livery. "So what are you gonna do?"

"Since I have an idea where they're goin'," Thomas said, swinging up into the saddle, "I don't have to track them. I can try to maybe get ahead of them."

"Might be you'll just catch up to the rest of your posse," Gibney said.

"Might be."

"Anybody else gonna be comin' along after you?"

Thomas briefly thought about his father, but he doubted Dan Shaye was ready to swing into the saddle just yet.

"I don't think so," he said.

"How long should I hold Davis?"

Thomas stared down at the man. "Until somebody comes for him."

"And somebody will?" Gibney asked. "You're sure?"

"I'm sure, Sheriff," Thomas said. "Somebody will come for him."

"Okay, then," Gibney said. "Good luck to you."

Thomas shook the man's hand, then gave the horse his heels and headed northeast.

54

Cardwell caught Jacks looking off into the darkness as they sat around their campfire.

"Look," he said, "if anyone's trackin' us, they're movin' slower than we are. We'll get where we're goin' before they catch up to us."

"That may be so," Jacks said, "but there's no reason we can't stay alert."

"Oh, I agree with that," Cardwell said. "In fact, why don't you stay alert first for about four hours, and then wake me."

"Yeah, okay," Jacks said, "I got first watch."

Cardwell nodded, then rolled himself up in his blanket and turned his back to Jacks.

"If we ride through the night we'll catch up to them," James said to Cory and Colon.

The two older men exchanged a glance.

"If we ride at night," Cory said, "it's more than likely one of our horses will step in a chuck hole and bust a leg. Then where will we be, huh?"

James had to admit he was right.

"Do not worry, my young friend," Colon said. "We will catch up to them."

"I know we will," James said. "I'm just worried about what'll happen when we do. If there's more than two of them . . ."

"We'll cross that bridge when we come to it, Deputy," Cory said. "Right now let's decide on the order of the watch, with your brother not bein' here."

James thought a moment, then said, "Ralph, you go first, then Berto, then me."

"Fine," Cory said. "You guys sleep tight."

James and Colon each went to their bedrolls and burrowed in. There was a chill in the air, but it wasn't bad. In fact, Cory liked it. It would help him keep his eyes open.

The ex-bounty hunter admitted something to himself when he was left alone with his thoughts. He actually enjoyed being back on the hunt. It made him feel alive again, and being able to read sign had come back to him quickly. The enjoyment he'd been getting from it was becoming harder and harder to hide from the others. He knew the feeling might change once they caught up to their prey, but that was later. For now, being back in the saddle was better than being behind the counter of any store. That was something he never would have guessed when he agreed to go along. He'd thought it was going to be a hell of a chore, but it wasn't. Not by a long sight.

* * *

Thomas considered riding through the night, but even though he might have caught up to his brother and the others that way, the risk to the horse wasn't worth it. He just didn't know the terrain well enough to take the chance. Instead, he made a cold camp so he could just up and leave at first light, making do with water and jerky.

He thought back to the few minutes he'd spent in the cell with Sean Davis. He wasn't particularly proud of himself for what he'd done, scaring the man half to death like that.

Davis swore up and down that he was just guessing when he told Thomas where he figured Ben Cardwell was headed. However, he was basing his guesses on things he'd heard Cardwell say over the past few months. Thomas decided to let the man keep his tongue and accept his guesses.

Now he took out his knife and stared at it. Would he have cut Davis's tongue out, as he had threatened? Probably not, but the mere fact that he'd used the threat didn't make him feel very good. He wondered what his pa would have thought if he'd been there to see it.

He put the knife away and took a bite of beef jerky. Not knowing the terrain would keep him from finding a shortcut and getting ahead of the others. Maybe if he could catch up to them quickly enough, though, Cory or Colon might know a quick route. Then again, rushing ahead to a place given him by Davis was putting more than a little faith in the man's guesses. If he was lying, or if he was wrong, they might lose track of the two men completely. Then he and James would have to go back to Vengeance Creek and admit their failure to their father.

Maybe he should just wait until he caught up to the others before making any more decisions.

Dan Shaye was unsure of himself.

He was camped, having built a fire so he could have some warm food and keep up his strength. But he was not sure he had done the right thing by leaving Vengeance Creek to go after his sons so long after they had left. What if they telegraphed, what if they needed him and he wasn't there? Instead, he was out here, wandering about aimlessly.

On top of that, his wound had started bleeding and he'd had to rewrap it. The doctor had warned him about infection, but he saw—and smelled— no evidence of any when he washed it and rebandaged it.

Shaye didn't like being unsure. He prided himself on remaining in control. But ever since the deaths of Mary and Matthew, he felt less and less in control.

As he saw it, he had two choices. He could either go back, or he could go forward, pushing himself at a faster pace. The trail was leading northeast, so what if he simply continued in that direction and didn't worry about reading sign? He was bound to come to a town where someone—

either the hunted or the hunters—had stopped. He could even telegraph Vengeance Creek himself and see if his sons had sent him any messages.

He finished his meal and had another cup of coffee before turning in. He'd break camp at first light and get back on the trail. He'd push hard and hope that his wound would not slow him down or worsen. Finding his sons alive and well was worth any risk.

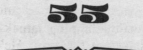

55

James decided on a cold breakfast, had Colon saddle all three horses quickly. They rode hard for most of the morning, but at one point, as the sun approached its zenith, James looked behind him and knew he saw something.

"Wait!" he said.

He reined in his horse and turned. The other two went on ahead a few yards, then came back.

"What is it?" Cory asked.

"This time I did see something."

Cory and Colon looked off into the distance but saw nothing.

"James," Cory said, "you're just seein'—"

"No," James said, "this time I'm right."

The terrain behind them was uneven, could have been hiding a rider from them. All three men continued to stare, and then James cried out, "There! See?"

"Berto?" Cory asked.

"I see it," Colon said. "A rider."

"It's Thomas!"

They continued to watch, and finally the rider came into full view. He was on a different horse, but it was Thomas.

"Yes," Cory said, slapping James on the back, "it's Thomas."

The three of them were dismounted by the time Thomas caught up to them. He swung down from his mount, approached his brother and stopped just short of hugging him.

"James."

"Thomas. It's about time you caught up."

"Actually," Cory said, "I think you made pretty good time."

"Fresh mount," Thomas said. "Back in Blue Mesa."

"Jesus," James said, "did you have to deal with that Scotsman? McShane?"

"Yeah," Thomas said, "but the sheriff helped me a bit."

"What happened with the Double W rancher?" Colon asked.

"Yeah," James said, "I forgot about that."

"Let's mount up and keep movin'," Thomas said. "I'll tell you about that, and about what I found out in Blue Mesa."

"From Davis?" James asked.

"Yes."

"He wasn't talkin' when we left," Colon said.

"I knew Thomas would get somethin' out of him," James said. "I knew it."

"Come on, little brother," Thomas said. "Let's keep movin'."

James, Colon, and Cory listened intently while Thomas told them of his conversations with Wendy Williams and Sean Davis.

"Well, too bad about the rancher," Cory said, "but did you believe Davis?"

"I did."

"Why?"

Thomas hesitated, then said, "Let's just say he wasn't in a position to lie to me."

"So if Cardwell and Jacks are going where Davis thinks they are, what should we do?" James asked.

"I don't know this area," Thomas said. He looked at Cory and Colon. "What about you two? Is there some way we could get there ahead of them?"

Cory and Colon exchanged a look, and then Colon shrugged and said, "I do not know."

"Ralph?"

"There might be," Cory said, "but if we do that and Davis is wrong, we'll lose them."

"I know that."

"So whose call is it gonna be?" Cory asked. "It's got to be one of you two."

"Let's give it some thought," Thomas said. "We can talk about it again when we make camp."

"Sounds good to me," James said.

Thomas looked at Cory and Colon.

"Fine by me."

"*Muy bien,*" Colon said. "I also agree."

"Okay then," Thomas said, "why don't you fellas tell me what you've been up to, then. . . ."

They brought Thomas up to date on what had happened since they split up. Among the things they mentioned was Sheriff Gibney thinking he had recognized "Ralph Cory."

"Yeah, he mentioned that to me too," Thomas said.

"Doesn't matter, really," Cory said. "I mean, it's not like I'm wanted or anything like that."

"Maybe not," James said, "but you don't really want people to know who you are either."

"No," Cory said, "but hey . . . there are other names, other places."

"No reason you can't go back to Vengeance Creek when this is all over," Thomas said.

"Maybe not," Cory said. "What about you fellas?"

"What about us?" James asked.

"You goin' back?"

"Sure," James said, "why not?"

Cory looked at Thomas, who looked away.

"Just a thought," Cory said. "I thought maybe you were havin' second thoughts."

"About what?"

"The law."

James laughed. "What else would we do?" He looked at Thomas for support, but found none there. "Thomas?"

"There are other things, James."

"What?" James said. "You're thinkin' about . . . givin' up the law?"

"Right now," Thomas said, "I'm thinkin' about gettin' this job done. Anything else can wait until we get back."

James looked as if wanted to say more, but in the end he simply fell silent.

Rigoberto Colon had observed the conversation between the other three but had stayed out of it. He had his own demons to deal with, which none of these men would understand. Dan Shaye had given him a reason to crawl out of the bottle. Now he had to decide whether he would crawl back in when this was all over. He had to admit that giving up the whiskey had not been as hard as he'd thought it would. Perhaps there had never really been a need for it at all.

They all rode in silence, alone with their own thoughts, until night began to fall and they made camp.

56

They went back to standing watches as they had since leaving Vengeance Creek, which meant Thomas went last. Toward daybreak he heard something snap behind him, turned to find James approaching.

"Hey," Thomas said, "it's early to be up. You've got about another hour."

"Couldn't sleep anymore," James said. "I'll make a fresh pot of coffee."

Thomas watched his brother prepare the coffee and still couldn't understand why it tasted different from his.

The night before, the four of them had discussed what they should do the next day. Cory was for continuing to track Cardwell and Jacks. After all, that was why he had been brought in. Colon was content to go along with whatever decision the others made. It was James who suggested that they should split up, two finding a shortcut and two continuing to track the bank robbers.

"That way we're covered no matter what happens."

"And once we get there," Cory had asked, "I mean, the two who go ahead, how long do we wait before we decide Davis was wrong and the other two aren't comin'?"

"All I'm sayin'," James answered, "is that we take the chance. Look, they're bound to have other guns waitin' for them. If we get there first—"

"And if they don't get there at all?" Cory interrupted. "The two of us who are still trackin' will be left high and dry."

"Okay," Thomas said. "Why don't we sleep on it and make our decision in the mornin'?"

"And who makes the decision then?" Cory asked, as he had that afternoon.

"James and I do," Thomas said. "We're wearing the badges."

"And why are Colon and I even talkin'?"

"We take your input into account, Ralph," Thomas had said.

"Right."

Cory looked at Colon. "You don't have much to say, Berto."

"What is there to say, amigo?" Colon replied with a shrug. "Thomas is right, they are wearing the badges. I am happy to sleep and wake to their decision."

"Fine," Cory said, "that's what we'll do, then."

Colon had looked at Thomas and James and said, "I just hope you make the right decision, *Jefes*."

Now, James handed Thomas a fresh cup of coffee, then poured one for himself and sat next to his brother.

"I think we should do what you said, James," Thomas said.

"What?"

"Split up. Two go ahead, and two keep trackin'."

"What made you decide that?"

Thomas shrugged. "It's as good an idea as any. If it works, we can cut them off before they join up with more men. If we have to face ten or twelve guns, we're gonna be way too outnumbered."

"And if they're not headed where Davis thinks?"

"Then we made a mistake," Thomas said, "and we'll have to live with it."

"We'll have to go home, tell Pa we failed," James said.

"Are you worried about Pa, or the mayor?"

"I'm not worried about the mayor," James said, "but I don't want Nancy's killer to get away."

"Neither do I, James."

"If we just stay on their trail, we should run them down eventually."

"Tryin' to get ahead of them was your idea."

"I know," James said, "but I'm havin' second thoughts."

"Then I have an idea."

"What's that?"

"I'll go ahead, and you stay on their trail."

"How are you gonna find a shortcut?"

"I'll take Cory with me. He's got the experience."

"And how are we supposed to continue to track them without him?" James asked.

"Berto can do it," Thomas said. "I think this is the best way to go, James. Cory and I go on ahead, you and Berto keep trackin'."

James stared at his brother for a few moments, then held his coffee cup out. "Agreed."

Thomas clinked his cup with his brother's and said, "Agreed."

"Now," James said, "let's talk about this business of you givin' up your badge."

"No."

"What? Thomas—"

"No, James," Thomas said. "That's somethin' to talk about when we get back, with Pa. Not now."

"Aw, Thomas—"

Thomas tossed the remains of his coffee into the fire and said, "I'm gonna wake the others."

He got up and walked away from the fire.

Over coffee and bacon Thomas told Cory and Colon what he and James had decided.

"We don't get a say?" Cory asked.

"It's like you yourself have said before, Ralph," Thomas said. "James and I are wearin' the badges."

"I just meant," Cory said, "Berto and I don't get any say about who goes with you and who goes with James."

"No," Thomas said. "You know the area, Ralph. You're the one who can take me to the shortcut."

"It may be a shortcut, but it won't be easy," Cory warned.

"What is?" Thomas asked.

After breakfast they each saddled their own mounts. They split what supplies they had, but James and Colon kept the coffee, and the only coffeepot.

Thomas and James faced each other.

"Splittin' up again," James said.

"It's gettin' to be a habit," Thomas replied. "With any luck, though, we'll see each other soon."

The two brothers shook hands and mounted up. James joined Colon, and they continued to follow the trail being left by Cardwell and Jacks.

"Okay," Thomas said to Cory, "which way?"

57

"Why are we stopping in Trinidad?" Jacks asked.

"We're pickin' someone up."

"I thought all the men were gonna be waitin' for us when we get there?"

"Not this one," Cardwell said. "This one's a special case."

"What's so special?"

Cardwell looked over at Jacks. "It's Durant."

Jacks immediately reined his horse in. Cardwell went on a few feet before he stopped his horse and turned it.

"Simon—"

"I won't work with Bart Durant," Jacks said.

"Jacks—"

"And you know he won't work with me," the other man went on. "How did you get him to agree— Oh, wait a minute. He doesn't know about me, does he?"

"No."

"He's not gonna go for this, Ben," Jacks said, "any more than I will. You know that."

"I think you both will," Cardwell said, "or you're both off of this job."

"Off the job?" Jacks repeated. "I don't even know what the job is."

"And neither does Durant," Cardwell said. "But when I tell you, you'll both agree to it."

"Not if it means workin' together, we won't."

"You wanna bet?"

Jacks hesitated, then asked, "How much?"

"Your end of the Vengeance Creek take against mine."

Jacks hesitated before saying, "You're that sure?"

"I'm that sure."

Jacks leaned back in his saddle, the leather creaking beneath him. If Cardwell was so sure, he didn't think he wanted to risk his end of the take to go against him.

"Okay . . ."

"It's a bet?"

"No bet," Jacks said, "but I'll listen. But I'll be shocked if you get Durant to listen."

"I won't be," Cardwell said.

"Why not?"

Cardwell turned his horse and said, "Because you listened, and I thought you were gonna be the hard one."

* * *

"Berto?"

"Sir?"

"You never seem to have any definite opinions about what we're doin'. Why is that?"

"Señor Shaye asked me to go along and help you and your brother," Colon explained. "That is what I am doing."

"Did you think this was a good idea?" James asked. "Splitting up like this?"

"It was your idea, no?"

"Yes, it was."

"And you are having the second thoughts about it?"

"Yes, I am."

Colon thought a moment, then shrugged. "It is as good an idea as any."

"That's what Thomas said."

"It will be like most ideas, I think."

"And how's that?"

"If it works, it will be a good idea," the Mexican said. "If it does not, it will be a bad one."

58

"Over the mountains?" Thomas asked. "That's your big shortcut?"

"It's the most direct route," Cory said. "If the horses are up to it, it'll get us there first."

"And if they're not?"

"One of us might end up stranded without a mount."

They were standing with their reins in their hands, staring up at the mountains.

"Are you sure about this?"

"Hey," Cory said, "you're the one who asked for the shortcut." He gestured to the mountain. "That's it."

"Maybe you should have told me this before we split from the others."

"And you would have changed your mind?"

"I don't know."

"Well, you can change it now, Thomas," Cory said. "I'm sure we can catch up to James and Berto."

Thomas thought a moment, then said, "No."

"So we'll go on?"

"Yeah, why not?" Thomas asked. "You've made this ride before, haven't you?"

"Well . . ."

Thomas looked at him. "You have, haven't you?"

"Well, I have. . . ."

"You want to explain that?"

"A few years ago I made the ride with, uh, two other men, but . . . uh, they didn't make it."

"What's so hard?" Thomas asked. "It's a mountain."

"It's not a clear path," Cory said. "And it's cold at the top . . . snowy."

"Are you tryin' to talk me out of this, Ralph?"

"No, Thomas," Cory said, "I'm just tellin' you it's not going to be easy."

"Okay," Thomas said. "I understand that. I've got it. Not gonna be easy. Right."

"Let's get mounted up, then," Cory said. "We have to get to a certain point and camp, so that when we do make it to the top, it's early in the day, not late."

"And how many days will it take?"

"That depends on conditions," Cory said. "We got an early start this morning, but by the time we get to the base of the mountain, it will be late. We'll have to camp there, camp again halfway up—"

"Okay, never mind," Thomas said. "Let's just get started."

* * *

It took them two days to get to the base of the mountain and camp.

"Why don't we start up? We've got plenty of daylight ahead of us," Thomas said.

"It's too late in the day," Cory told him. "We'll camp here and start up at first light."

Thomas looked up. From his vantage point, the mountain didn't look that steep.

"Don't let it fool you, Thomas," Cory said. "It's gonna look a lot steeper when you're lookin' down."

Thomas had noticed a week ago that Cory's speech pattern was changing. He no longer sounded like "Ralph Cory," the owner of a store in Vengeance Creek. His speech had become more western, and he sounded more like himself and James now.

"What?" Cory asked as they unsaddled their horses.

"I—uh, you're just, uh, talkin' kinda different."

"When you take on a different name, you also take on a different way of talkin', and of livin'," Cory said. "Out here, I'm not tryin' to fool anybody anymore."

"It must be hard," Thomas said, "always tryin' to remember to be someone else."

"You get used to it, after a while," Cory said, "but it's hard in the beginning."

"You can go back, you know," Thomas said. "After this is all over. My pa and us, we're not gonna tell anybody. Berto won't say nothin' either."

"I know," Cory said. "I know that. It's just somethin' I'm gonna have to decide."

Thomas suddenly turned and faced Cory. "Ralph," he said, "are you . . . likin' this?"

Cory stopped what he was doing, hung his head for a moment, then looked at the younger man.

"Yeah, Thomas," he said, "yeah, I'm pretty sure I am . . . but it ain't gonna last."

"Whataya mean?"

"Before we're done," Cory said, "I'm gonna have to kill somebody. You know it, and I know it."

"And that was the part you were tryin' to get away from."

Cory nodded.

"Ralph—"

"Forget it, Thomas," Cory said. "Just forget it. I get the feelin' that by the time this is done, we're all gonna have some thinkin' to do."

59

As Thomas and Cory reached the base of their mountain, Cardwell and Jacks arrived in the town of Trinidad, not far north of the Colorado border.

"You know," Jacks said, just as an observation, "we could head south into New Mexico, get lost there for a while."

"I'm not givin' up my bank, Simon," Cardwell said. "I been wantin' to hit this one for a long time, and now I'm gonna do it. After that, we could retire to New Mexico if we wanted to."

Cardwell had been dangling that carrot in front of Jacks for days now. But the addition of Bart Durant to the mix was making Jacks unhappy. He hated Durant, and knew the man returned the feeling. The two would just as soon shoot each other as look at each other. There was going to have to be a lot of money involved to change that.

A helluva lot.

"Hey, wasn't Bat Masterson the law here for a while?" Jacks asked.

" 'Bout eight years ago, I think," Cardwell said, "in 1882, but I don't think he was even here a year."

"Wonder where he is now?"

"Denver, I think," Cardwell said, "but not wearin' a badge."

They rode into the center of town, which was bustling with activity. Folks were rushing to stores and the bank before closing time, and women were rushing home to get supper ready for their men and their families. Children were happy to be out of school and were enjoying their temporary freedom.

"Where's Durant supposed to meet us?" Jacks asked.

"The Columbian Hotel."

"Where's that?"

Cardwell reined his horse to a halt and said, "Right there," with a jerk of his chin.

The Columbian was on the corner of Main and Commercial, and had been built eleven years ago, in 1879.

"Looks expensive."

"We can afford it."

"We?" Jacks asked. "You think I'm payin' for Durant's room in that hotel—"

"Okay, okay," Cardwell said, "it'll come out of my end. You happy now?"

"Yeah, I'm happy."

"Come on," Cardwell said, "let's get the horses cared for, and then we'll find Durant and get this over with."

* * *

"One hour," Rigoberto Colon said, holding some of the dirt in his hand.

"We're closin' on them," James said. "Damn. If Thomas and Ralph had stayed—"

"We cannot worry about that now," Colon said, mounting up again. "We must decide what to do if we catch up to them."

"There's no question," James said. "We'll take 'em."

Colon didn't reply.

"You got another idea, Berto?"

"I was just thinkin', *Jefe*."

"About what?"

"They have changed direction."

"Whataya mean?"

"They are going more east now, not so much north."

"Which means?'

"One of two things."

"I'm listening, Berto."

"They are probably going to Trinidad."

"What's there?"

"Supplies," Colon said. "Also, if they go to Trinidad and then head north, they avoid going over the mountains."

"So they're takin' the long way around."

"*Sí.*"

"Which works for us if we're right about where they're heading," James said.

"*Sí,*" Colon said again.

"But you said two things."

Colon looked at James. "Perhaps they still stop in Trinidad and then go south."

"Which means Thomas and Ralph are goin' the wrong way."

"*Sí.*"

James thought a moment, then said, "Well, either way, they're headin' for Trinidad, right?"

"It would appear so."

"And how long will it take us to get there?"

"About an hour."

"Let's go, then," James said. "If they're there when we get there, we can decide what to do."

"And if not," Colon said, "if they have already left, we'll know whether they are riding north or south."

"Yeah."

As they headed toward Trinidad, James was acutely aware that his brother was up on a mountain because of his idea. If the bank robbers headed south, Thomas was going to be completely out of this hunt, and it would fall to him to apprehend them and bring them back.

Or kill them.

Suddenly, he wished he had "Ralph Cory" with him rather than Berto Colon.

60

"What mountains are these?" Thomas asked as he passed Cory a hunk of beef jerky. They had no coffee, but had built a fire for the warmth. They were washing down their beef jerky dinner with swallows of water from their canteens.

"The Sangre de Cristo Mountains," Cory said. "When we get to the other side you'll see the Spanish Peaks."

"Spanish Peaks?" Thomas asked. "We have to go over more mountains?"

"No," Cory said, "we're gonna go north of the peaks to the old Taos Trail. In fact, we don't even have to go to the top of these mountains."

"Why not?"

"We can take the Sangre de Cristo Pass. It's a branch of the old Sante Fe Trail."

"So goin' over may not be as rough as you said."

"Maybe not," Cory said. "The passes just have to be open. I haven't been there in a lot of years."

Thomas took a bite from his beef jerky and sat

back, wondering where James was at that moment and what he was doing. If he and Colon managed to catch up to Cardwell and Jacks, and something happened . . . well, he'd have a lot of explaining to do to his father about why they split up.

Thomas looked over at Cory and found the man staring up the mountain.

"Ralph?"

"Hm? Oh, I was just thinkin' . . . I've been doin' a lot of things lately I thought I was done with."

"You mean like ridin' over a mountain?"

"Yeah," Cory said. "I thought I'd be spending the rest of my life behind the counter of some store. I'm too old to be doin' this."

"You're my pa's age," Thomas said. "That ain't too old."

"No?" Cory asked. "Ask your pa next time you see him how old he feels, especially when he's in the saddle."

"You seem to be doin' okay."

"My ass is killin' me, Thomas," Cory said.

"But you told me you were enjoyin' it."

"Some of it, yeah," Cory said. "Readin' sign is somethin' I've always gotten satisfaction from doin'. It's like this writing in the ground that only some people can read, you know?"

Thomas nodded. He didn't know, so there was no point in commenting.

"And my ass ain't hurtin' as much as it was,"

Cory went on. "But I'll know more about myself once we get over this mountain."

"And then when we get where we're goin'?" Thomas asked.

Cory looked down at the gun on his hip, and then touched it.

"Yeah," he said, "that's when we'll really see."

Thomas sat forward and stared at Cory.

"Ralph," he said, "You gotta tell me now if you're gonna be able to use your gun when the time comes. I've gotta know if you're gonna be able to cover my back."

"Thomas," Cory said, "I'll cover your back better than anyone you know, but I don't know what's gonna happen after that."

Thomas knew he should be concerned with the man's well-being, but he was more concerned with catching these men after tracking them for weeks. Maybe there'd be more guilt for him when this was all over, but he'd have to deal with it then. There was a lot to be settled when this hunt was all over, so how could it hurt to have one more?

He sat back against his saddle and said, "Okay, then."

"Okay," Cory said. "You want first watch, or should I take it?"

"Who's gonna come up on us from behind?" Thomas asked. "Or from this mountain?"

"Thomas," Cory said, "we've gotten into the habit of settin' watches. That's not a habit you want to break right now."

"You're right," Thomas said. "I'll take the first watch. I'm not ready to sleep yet."

"That's because you're young," Cory said. "I'm ready to sleep for days."

"Good," Thomas said. "I'll wake you in four hours."

61

Cardwell and Jacks entered the lobby of the Columbian Hotel in Trinidad, Colorado. The lobby was busy, but there was no sign of Bart Durant.

"Where is he?"

"Relax," Cardwell said, hefting his saddlebags up on his shoulder. "He'll be here. Let's get a room."

"Rooms," Jacks said, tapping his own saddlebags. "I want my own this time."

"Fine."

They walked to the front desk, where the clerk gave them a dubious look. They were covered with trail dust from days in the saddle and sleeping on the ground.

"Can I help you?"

"Two rooms," Cardwell said.

"And baths?" the man asked.

"What are you, a wise—" Jacks started, but Cardwell put his hand on his colleague's arm.

"Sure," he said, "we'll want baths. After all, I'm sure we look terrible."

"Well," the clerk said, relenting, "I'm sure you've been traveling for quite some time."

He turned the register around so they could each sign in, then handed them keys to rooms that were right across from each other.

"I'll have your baths drawn," he added.

"Thank you."

Cardwell led Jacks to the stairs.

"Why the hell did you let him talk down to us like that?" Jacks demanded.

"We don't want to attract any attention, Simon," Cardwell said. "And baths are a good idea. We stink."

Jacks lifted his sleeve and sniffed himself, then made a face. "Yeah, I guess you're right."

They went up the stairs and stopped outside their rooms.

"You go for your bath first," Cardwell said, "and I'll find Durant."

"Why don't I go with you?"

"Because you guys might slap leather as soon as you see each other," Cardwell said. "I need to talk to him first."

"You got a point there."

They unlocked their doors, but before entering the room, Cardwell looked up and down the hallway and said, "Hey."

"What?"

"Don't take your saddlebags down to your bath."

"I ain't leavin' them—"

"Hey," Cardwell said, "how's it gonna look if you take saddlebags with you to take a bath?"

"Like I want to keep them near me."

"Yeah," Cardwell said, "like you got somethin' in them that's worth a lot of money."

"Like I *got* a lot of money in them."

"Exactly," Cardwell said. "You might as well tell everyone what you're carrying."

"So what do you expect me to do?"

"Leave it in your room."

"Wha—"

Cardwell closed the door to his room, stepped across the hall and pushed Jacks into his room, closing the door behind them.

"Nobody knows what we have," he said urgently. "We can both leave our bags in our rooms while we take baths and talk to Durant."

"You're gonna leave yours in your room?" Jacks asked.

"Yes."

"I don't believe it."

"I tell you what," Cardwell said, slinging his bags off his shoulder, "I'll leave them in your room."

"What?"

"Sure, why not?" Cardwell asked. "You hold onto all the money."

Jacks narrowed his eyes. "Why would you trust me?"

"Because there's a lot more money waitin' for us," Cardwell said, "and I don't think you want to miss out on it . . . do you?"

"No, I don't, but . . ."

"But what?"

Cardwell held his saddlebags out to Jacks, who finally reached out and took them. .

"Stick them under the bed," he suggested. "That's probably as safe a place as any. We'll only be overnight, nobody's gonna steal anythin' from us."

Cardwell opened the door. "I'm just gonna wash my face and hands in my room, and then go look for Durant."

"I'll take my bath," Jacks said, "and then come right back up here."

"Good," Cardwell said, "then I'll meet you back here."

After Cardwell left, Simon Jacks put both sets of saddlebags on the bed and opened Cardwell's. Sure enough, it was stuffed with money. He'd thought maybe Cardwell had taken the money out and replaced it with something else, but apparently the man actually was trusting him with all the money.

That was extremely out of character for him.

62

Cardwell waited until Jacks had gone down to take his bath before leaving his room and going downstairs. He went across the lobby and into the saloon adjoining it. There he found Bart Durant, whom he'd telegraphed from Bene Mesa, sitting at a table with a beer. Cardwell walked over and sat across from him.

"Where is he?" Durant asked.

"Takin' a bath."

"Does he have his gun with him?"

"Of course."

"And the money?"

"In his room."

"Your share and his?"

"Yes."

Durant sat back in his chair. He was a morose-looking man in his forties who had been making his way with his gun for more than half his life. He and Simon Jacks had hated each other for a long time. Ben Cardwell didn't know why, and he didn't care. He was simply prepared to use that hatred to his advantage.

"I get his share," Durant said.

"That's right."

"And I'm in on the big job?"

"That's right," Cardwell said. "All you have to do is meet me there . . . after."

"And the money?"

"It'll be in his room," Cardwell said, "under the bed."

Durant studied Cardwell for a few moments, then said, "Okay."

"Just give me time to retrieve my share, get on my horse, and ride out," Cardwell said, "then he's all yours."

Cardwell stood up.

"You really think the money's gonna be there?" Durant asked.

"Mine, or yours?"

"Oh," Durant said, "mine better be there."

"It'll be there, Durant," Cardwell said. "You just better take care of Jacks."

"I've been waitin' to take care of Simon Jacks for years," Durant said. "I ain't about to miss my chance."

"Then I'll see you soon," Cardwell said.

Durant nodded and lifted his beer mug. Cardwell turned and left the saloon. He went upstairs, forced the door on Jacks's room, retrieved his saddlebags from beneath the bed, went outside, mounted his horse, and rode out of town.

He headed north.

James and Colon rode into Trinidad from one end as Ben Cardwell was riding out the other.

"Where do we look?" James said aloud.

"The livery," Colon said. "We find the horse with the track, and then we find the man who belongs to the horse."

"Simple as that, huh?"

Colon looked at James and grinned. "*Sí, Jefe,* simple as that."

They were riding past the Columbian Hotel when all hell seemed to break loose. . . .

Durant finished his beer, then slid his chair back, stood and walked into the lobby. He walked to the front desk and got the clerk's attention.

"Where are the bathtubs?"

"Down that hall, sir," the clerk said. "I can have one drawn for you. Are you a guest of the hotel?"

"No," Durant said, "I just want to surprise an old friend."

"Sir, I can't let you—" the clerk started, but then he saw the money Durant was holding out to him. "Yes, of course, sir. I hope he's very surprised."

"Don't worry," Durant said, "he will be."

Simon Jacks hated taking baths, so he took quick ones. He left his gun belt hanging on a chair next to the tub when he got in, so the gun was within easy reach. He was still feeling uneasy about Cardwell giving him all the money to hold. It just didn't sit right—and yet leaving the saddlebags in the room made sense to him. A man holding his saddlebags too close at all times would certainly look like someone who had something valuable. That was all some men would need to target him, and Cardwell was right, they didn't need the attention.

But he bathed extra fast so he could get back to his room, where all the money from the Vengeance Creek job was underneath the bed. He was pulling on his trousers when he heard a floorboard creak outside the door. He grabbed his gun belt, freed the gun just as the door slammed open.

"Durant!" he shouted.

In that moment he knew he'd been betrayed. He was supposed to be in the tub, up to his neck in water when Durant burst in. An easy target for his hated enemy.

Durant looked shocked as Jacks raised his gun. But the man had quick reflexes, and before Jacks could fire, he backed out of the room and ran down the hall toward the lobby.

Shoeless, Jacks chased him. He knew he had to finish Durant quick and get to Cardwell before the man could leave town.

He ran out into the hall, dropped to his knees as Durant fired two quick shots at him before running out into the lobby. Jacks chased him, came out into the lobby as people were scrambling for cover.

Durant turned in the middle of the lobby and fired at Jacks. One bullet struck the wall behind Jacks, while the other plowed into the desk clerk. As the man fell to the floor, Jacks stepped over him and returned fire.

"Damn you, Durant!" he shouted. "Damn you!"

Durant was furious. Things had not gone as planned, and he blamed Cardwell for that. If he hadn't had to wait long enough for the man to get out of town, Jacks would have been easy pickings in the tub. He also blamed Jacks for taking such a quick bath. Didn't the man know baths were for soaking in?

People were running through the lobby or simply hitting the floor to get out of the way of flying lead. Durant had two choices. He could run upstairs and go after the money, or head out into the street—but what if the money wasn't there? No, the best thing to do was take care of Jacks first and then go for the money.

He decided to take the fight out into the street. Jacks had no boots on, and that might be an advantage.

He turned and went out the front door, firing two shots behind him for cover . . .

* * *

James and Colon heard the shots and reined their horses in. Suddenly, the front door of the hotel began belching out people.

"What the hell—" James said.

"Dismount!" Colon shouted.

Both men dropped from their horses and drew their guns just as a man with a gun came running out of the hotel, firing wildly behind him.

"Berto."

Colon put his hand on James's arm. "Wait."

The man with the gun reached the street and turned around, waiting for someone. At that moment a second man came through the door, shoeless, gun in hand. He spotted the man in the street and both men began firing at the same time. The man in the street got the worst of it as two bullets slammed into his chest. James and Colon saw blood spurt from his back as the bullets went right through him. The man's gun flew from his hand as he fell onto his back in the dirt.

Jacks put two bullets into Durant's chest, and he'd never felt such satisfaction before. As the man fell onto his back, he saw two men watching, and one of them was wearing a badge. He recognized him from Vengeance Creek. It was one of the Shaye deputies. Jesus, had they trailed him here?

Jacks knew he was never going to get a chance at that sonofabitch Cardwell unless he got through this deputy. The man was just staring, not sure of what was happening. Jacks realized that while he knew who the deputy was, the young lawman did not know him.

He had to take the boy out while he had the chance. . . .

"What the hell was that about?" James asked.

"I do not know," Colon said.

James started as the man fired in their direction. He heard Colon grunt and go down, looked over and saw him holding his shoulder. He grabbed for his own gun as the man pulled the trigger again. He didn't find out later that the only thing that had saved his life was that Jacks's gun was empty. He didn't know that, however, when he pulled the trigger of his own gun and shot Simon Jacks in the chest.

63

It was deathly quiet on the street once the shooting stopped. Then James heard the sound of men running. When he turned, he saw three men with badges advancing on him, their guns out. Instantly, he put his hands in the air, his gun still in his right.

"It's all over!" he shouted. "It's over!"

"Drop the gun!" the man wearing the sheriff's badge hollered back. "Drop it!"

"Easy! Take it easy," James said. "I'm a lawman." He looked down at Colon, who was holding his hand over his shoulder, ribbons of blood running through his fingers. "My friend needs a doctor."

"Drop the gun, I said."

James obeyed, dropping his pistol to the ground. The lawman took in the picture before him, then said to his deputies, "Check on those other two."

"Right, Sheriff," one of them said.

The lawman was tall, square-shouldered, with a face that looked as if it had been carved from granite.

"I'm Sheriff Sam Dean. Identify yourself," he said.

"I'm Deputy James Shaye, from Vengeance Creek, Arizona."

"Arizona?" The man frowned. "You're a little out of your jurisdiction. Let me see your badge."

James moved his arms so the man could see his badge.

"Toss it over here."

James hesitated, then took it off and tossed it to the man, who caught it deftly in his left hand. The sheriff looked at it, then put it in his pocket.

"Hey!" James protested.

"You'll get it back . . . when I'm sure it's yours."

James was going to protest again, but a groan from Rigoberto Colon changed his mind.

"My friend needs a doctor."

"He's with you?"

"Yes."

"Also a deputy?"

"No, he's just . . . with me."

"Part of your posse, I suppose?"

"That's right."

"Sheriff," one of the deputies said, "they're both dead."

"That one killed that one," James said, pointing, "and I killed him."

"Who are they?" the sheriff asked.

"Can we get him to a doctor, please?" James asked.

The sheriff relented and said to the deputy, "All right, Hal, take him over to the doc."

"You don't want me to stay—"

"Just walk him to the doc's."

"Yes, sir."

As the deputy bent over to help Colon up, the sheriff said, "And take his gun!"

"Yes, sir."

The lawman turned his attention back to James. "You know these two?"

"The one in front of the hotel is probably Simon Jacks."

"Jacks?"

"You know him?"

"I've heard of him. And the other one?"

"I don't know him."

"Then why did you kill him?"

James took a deep breath. "I didn't kill him," he said, "I killed Jacks—if it is Jacks."

"You're not sure?"

"No, I'm not."

"But you killed him anyway."

"He shot my . . . my partner."

"Sheriff?" It was the other deputy.

"Yeah, Ted."

"That one by the door, his gun was empty."

"It wasn't empty," James said, "he just fired all his shots."

"That means it was empty," the sheriff said.

"I didn't know that when I fired back."

"Ted, get some men to help get these fellas off the street," Dean said. "I'm gonna take the . . . the *deputy* here over to the office. See if anybody knows who they are."

"Yes, sir."

"Ask the desk clerk," Dean said. "Maybe one of them is a registered guest."

"I can't do that, Sheriff."

"Why not?"

"Uh, the clerk's dead."

Sheriff Dean looked at James.

"Don't look at me," James said. "I didn't kill him. I never went inside."

"Okay," the sheriff said, "okay, just get the bodies off the street, Ted."

"Yes, Sheriff."

"All right, Deputy," Dean said. "Walk ahead of me and we'll finish discussing this in my office."

64

James stared out from between the bars of his cell in disbelief. The sheriff had tossed his badge—*his* badge—into a desk drawer and deposited him in a cell.

"Once I've verified with the sheriff of Vengeance Creek that you're who you say you are, I'll let you out and give you back your badge. Until then . . . what would you like for dinner?"

"Sheriff," James said, "this is ridiculous. It could take days to get an answer—"

"Didn't you tell me the sheriff was your pa?"

"That's right, but—"

"Then he should respond to my telegraph message real quick, don't ya think?"

"Sheriff, do you have any kids?"

"No," the man said. "My wife died before we could have kids, and I never remarried. Fifty-five years old and all I got is my job."

James didn't want to start discussing the sheriff's life with him. "And I'm sure you do a fine job . . . do you have any brothers?" James asked hopefully.

"No," Dean said, "never had no brothers or sisters."

This wasn't going to be easy, but James knew he had to try anyway.

"Sheriff, my brother is gonna have to face Ben Cardwell and whatever crew he gathers together alone if I don't get out of here and back on the trail."

"You'll be out as soon as I get my reply," Dean said. "Not before."

"Did you at least identify the two dead men?"

"Yeah, we did," Dean said. "The one you killed registered as Simon Jacks. I know who he is, and he wasn't wanted in this state. The other man resembles a poster I got on a fella called Bart Durant."

"I don't know that name."

"He was wanted here and in New Mexico, but since you didn't kill him, you don't get any reward, and the man who did kill him is already dead."

So Sheriff Dean was probably going to claim the reward on the dead outlaw. But James didn't care about that at the moment.

"Did you check Jacks's room?"

"We did," Dean said. "We found an empty set of saddlebags under his bed."

"Empty?"

"That's right. Steak okay for you for dinner? They do a great steak over at the café—"

"Sonofabitch."

"What?"

"Cardwell," James said. "I'll bet that son-ofabitch set these two men against each other so he could ride off with the entire haul from the Vengeance Creek bank."

"That could be," Dean said, rubbing his strong jaw. "Ain't no honor among thieves, ya know."

"Sheriff, look," James said, pleading, "we're both lawmen, how about some professional courtesy—"

"I'll give you all the professional courtesy you want," Dean said, "once I'm sure you're who you say you are."

"What about my friend?"

"He took a bullet in the shoulder," Dean said. "Doc's patchin' him up, but he ain't goin' nowhere soon. In fact, I may just put him in that cell next to you."

"What did he do?" James asked. "Besides get shot?"

"He rode in with you, and I don't know who you or he is," Dean said. "Until I do, I think I'll just keep the both of you where I can keep an eye on you."

"Sheriff," James said, "if anythin' happens to my brother, you're gonna have to answer not only to me, but to my pa—"

"Steak, I think," Dean said. "I'll get you and your friend steak for dinner."

"Sheriff!" James shouted, but the man left the cell block and closed the door behind him.

James could only hope that his father would respond to Sheriff Dean's telegraph message as soon as he got it. Good thing his pa had stayed behind.

Dan Shaye rode up on some men working on a fence, and they all turned to look up at him. It wasn't that hot, but he was sweating heavily. His wound had started to bleed a few miles back, or maybe more.

"Afternoon," he said.

"What can we do for you, friend?" one man asked.

"My name's Dan Shaye," he said, steadying himself in his saddle. "I'm sheriff of a town called Vengeance Creek."

"I'm Hal Forbes," the other man said. "Foreman of the Double W ranch."

"Double W?" Shaye asked.

"Say," Forbes said before Shaye could go on, "you wouldn't be kin to a Thomas Shaye, would ya? Well, sure ya would, 'cause he was wearin' a deputy's badge when he came by."

"You saw Thomas?"

"Yeah, him and three others," Forbes said. "One was his brother?"

"My other son, James," Shaye said. "When were they here?"

"Oh, some time back, I reckon," Forbes said. "They were trailin' some murderin' bank robbers."

"That's right," Shaye said, "and I'm trailin' them."

"Sheriff Shaye," Forbes said, "you don't mind me sayin', you don't look too good . . . and is that blood soakin' into the leg of your pants?"

Shaye swayed in his saddle and said, "I could use a little help, I guess . . . bandage . . . telegraph?"

"We can help with both. . . . Hey, hey, catch him boys, he's fallin'!"

65

Ben Cardwell believed that everything had gone according to plan. Sean Davis had been left behind, and now Simon Jacks had been taken care of by Bart Durant. With any luck, Durant had also been taken care of by either Jacks or the local law.

He was in the clear.

He now had all the money from the Vengeance Creek bank job in his saddlebags, having left the empty set under the bed in Jacks's room. Even if Durant got away from Trinidad and came looking for him, he'd never find him. Once he completed this last job, he'd have enough money to disappear for good.

Ben Cardwell had the supreme arrogance to believe that no one could touch him. Not the many partners he had double-crossed and left behind, and not the law. He was too smart for all of them, as evidenced by the fact that he was now riding alone, with all the money from Vengeance Creek.

He was heading north, with the intention of hitting the one bank he'd always wanted to hit—the Bank of Denver.

The Sangre de Cristo Pass was clear, which was good news for Thomas and Cory. The horses had made it fine, and Cory was pleased with his own performance.

"Maybe you're not as old as you think," Thomas said across the fire.

"Oh, yeah," Cory said, "I'm as old as I think, but I'm in better shape than I thought."

Thomas looked up at the moon, and the peaks silhouetted against them.

"Those are beautiful."

"Las Cumbras Espanolas," Cory said, "as our friend Rigoberto would say."

"And what would we say?"

"The Spanish Peaks."

"Right, right," Thomas said, "the mountains we don't have to go over."

"It shouldn't be very hard from here," Cory said, washing down some jerky with water from his canteen. They had found a waterhole and had been able to refill the canteens with some ice cold mountain water.

"I hope James is all right," Thomas said.

"Maybe you've got to stop takin' care of him, Thomas," Cory said. "Let him go off on his own sometime."

"This was sometime, Ralph," Thomas said.

"This is the first time James and I have been out without Pa. I've got to look after him. If somethin' happens to him, I'm gonna have to explain it to Pa."

"Well, he's got Rigoberto with him."

"Considering Pa pulled Berto out of the back room of a saloon, that don't make me feel too confident."

"Berto's a good man, Thomas," Cory said. "Don't worry. When they get to Denver, we'll be there waitin'."

"Hopefully ahead of Cardwell and Jacks," Thomas said. "If he gets there first and manages to put some men together, we'll be outnumbered."

"I've been outnumbered before," Cory said. "From what you told me about last year, you and your brother and your pa have been too."

"Yeah, we have."

"Get some sleep," Cory said. "I'll take the first watch tonight. It's been a long time since I've been here. I want to sit back and enjoy it for a while."

"Sounds good to me," Thomas said, pulling his blanket around him. "I'm beat."

"Yeah," Cory said, "you better rest your young bones while the old-timer stands watch."

"Fine," Thomas said through a yawn, "whatever you say . . . old-timer."

* * *

When Dan Shaye opened his eyes, he looked around at the unfamiliar surroundings. He didn't think he had ever been in a bed, or a room, this plush and comfortable. Frowning, he tried to remember how he had gotten there.

He tossed back the blanket and looked down at himself. He was naked, except for a clean new bandage on his wound. When he heard the doorknob turn, he quickly covered himself before the door opened.

"Oh good," the woman who entered said, "you're awake."

"Who are you?" he demanded. "How did I get here?"

"My name is Wendy Williams," the attractive young woman said, "and you're in my home. This is the Double W Ranch."

"Double—I remember. I was talking to a man—your foreman—"

"Hal Forbes," she said, smoothing down the front of her blue dress and perching herself on the edge of the bed. She smelled like lilacs. He knew that because his wife, Mary, had loved lilacs. "Yes, my foreman. You were talking to him and some of my men when you fell off your horse. They brought you here, and I had the doctor from town come and look at you."

"What did he say?"

"He said that judging from the severity of your wound—which he judges to be anywhere from ten days to two weeks old—you should not be riding a horse."

"I have to ride," he said. "I have to find my sons."

"Thomas being one of them?" she asked.

"Yes, and James."

"Your sons . . . and your deputies?"

"Yes."

"Have you not heard from them since they left Vengeance Creek to track those bank robbers?"

"No, I haven't."

She frowned and said, "Not very considerate of them not to have sent you a telegram, at least."

"No, it wasn't."

"Or could it be they're just doing their job, the way you taught them?"

Shaye looked at the woman sharply, then relaxed and said, "You're a very smart young woman, aren't you, ma'am?"

"I like to think so," she said, "and please don't call me ma'am. My name is Wendy."

"Well, Wendy, I thank you for your help, and I'd like to have my clothes now so I can be on my way."

"No."

"I— What?"

"I may not be able to keep you from riding," she said, standing up, "but I can keep you from riding anymore today. In the morning, if you still want to go, I'll bring you some clothes. You'll have to wear a pair of my father's old pants. Yours were soaked with blood, and we had to cut them off you."

Shaye studied the determined set of the young woman's chin for a moment and knew he was licked.

"Can you at least have someone go to town and send a telegram for me?"

"I can do that," she said. "I'll get you some paper and pencil so you can write it out."

"I'm much obliged to you, ma—Wendy."

"I'll be right back," she said, "with pencil, paper . . . and some food. And if you don't eat it, I won't loan you a pair of my father's pants."

As she left the room, Shaye had to admit that he was feeling hungry. Some food and a good night's rest in a plush bed like this one would do him a world of good, and then he could hit the trail again early the next morning.

When she returned and set a tray of stew by his bed—after eliciting from him the promise to eat it—he wrote out his telegram for her to have sent to Vengeance Creek for him. He hoped it would cross wires with something from one or both of his sons, so he could know where they were and how they were.

He never would have guessed the response he'd receive.

66

When Thomas and Ralph Cory finally rode into Denver, they were tired, hungry, dirty, and bearded.

"First thing we've got to do is talk to the local law," Thomas said.

"That would be the police," Cory said. "They have a police department here, like in the East."

"No sheriff?"

"Oh, there's a sheriff, but he's not a sheriff like your pa is," Cory said. "No, we have to talk to the chief of police—but before we do that we'll have to clean up, or he won't even see us."

"What if Cardwell's already here?"

"We'll have to hope he's not," Cory said. "We have to hope we didn't come over the mountains and through the pass for no reason at all. But either way, I'm tellin' you the police chief won't see us lookin'—and smellin'—like this."

"All right," Thomas said. "We'll take baths, get

shaved, and then go see him. Can we do that without actually checking into a hotel?"

"We could," Cory said, "but checkin' into a hotel sounds like a good idea to me. We're likely gonna have to spend a few nights here, no matter what happens."

"Ralph," Thomas said, "we should probably get right over to the bank and warn them."

"Thomas, do you know which bank Cardwell wants to hit?"

"Davis told us," Thomas replied. "The Bank of Denver."

"Do know how many banks are in Denver?" Cory asked. "Do you know how many of them are called the Bank of Denver?"

"There's more than one?"

"Oh, yes, there's more than one."

"Then . . . how will we know which one Cardwell's gonna hit?" Thomas asked, suddenly feeling very helpless.

"We'll discuss it with the chief of police," Cory said. "He can probably tell us which bank is the biggest. Or will have the most money on hand. If Cardwell's been waiting his whole rotten career to hit this bank, it'll probably be the biggest."

"But before the chief will see us . . ."

"Right," Cory said, "bath and shave. Come on, we'll check into the closest hotel."

"Will they have baths?"

"Thomas," Cory said, "in this city all the hotels have baths—in your room!"

"Right in the room?" Thomas said. "No."

Later, after they'd secured a room, had a bath and a shave, and paused to have a drink to wash the trail dust out of their throats, they went to police headquarters on Cherokee Street and asked to speak with the chief of police.

The uniformed policeman at the front desk asked, "What's it about?"

"A bank robbery."

"Where did this take place?"

"It hasn't happened yet," Thomas said. They'd agreed he would do the talking, since he was the one wearing a badge.

The officer, a big, florid-faced man in his fifties, stared at him and asked, "Then how do you know it's gonna happen?"

"Look," Thomas said, "my name is Thomas Shaye, I'm a deputy sheriff from Vengeance Creek, Arizona, and I've tracked a bank robber and killer to your city. I think he's gonna hit another bank here."

"Which one?'

"The Bank of Denver."

"Son," the man said, "we have a lot of Banks of Denver—' "

"I think if I could speak with the chief of police we could get this cleared up."

The man thought this over while Thomas inspected the gold and silver badge on his uniformed chest that said DENVER POLICE. Finally, the man said, "Wait a minute," and picked up the receiver of a telephone on his desk. Thomas had only seen a telephone once before, in Oklahoma City, and he'd never used one. Denver also offered him a second look at trolleys and electric lights, things he'd also only seen the year before during his brief and deadly stay in Oklahoma City.

"All right," the officer said, "the chief says he'll see you. Wait here and someone will come for you."

With that, the officer proceeded to ignore them.

"This might not be easy," Thomas said.

"What is?" Cory asked. "Just don't back down, Thomas. Be confident."

Thomas nodded just as a young officer came out and asked, "Deputy Shaye?"

"That's right."

"Come with me, please?"

"All right." Thomas and Cory started forward.

"Uh, who's this?"

"He's with me," Shaye said.

"And your name?"

"Ralph Cory."

"Are you a deputy?"

"I'm a volunteer."

The young policeman hesitated, then said, "All right. Follow me."

They trailed him down a long hall to a closed door with gold lettering that proclaimed: OFFICE OF THE CHIEF OF POLICE. The young man knocked, opened the door and announced, "Deputy Shaye and Mr. Ralph Cory."

He stepped aside to allow Thomas and Cory to enter.

That same morning, sixty-seven miles away in Colorado Springs, Ben Cardwell sat in a café with four men.

"You four are hired, and you have to bring in eleven more men. This is a job that'll take a dozen of us."

The four men exchanged a glance, and then Scott Dolan said, "We can do that."

"By tomorrow mornin'," Cardwell said.

This time there was hesitation, but Dolan said, "All right."

"Saddled up and ready to go at first light. I want to be in Denver by tomorrow night."

"That'll take some hard ridin'," Dolan said.

"So get me eleven men who can ride hard," Cardwell said.

"We're gonna need some money to outfit."

Cardwell had come prepared. He had a couple of packs of Vengeance Creek money folded into a newspaper on the table. Now he pushed the newspaper across to Dolan.

"There should be enough in there to do the job."

Dolan put his hand on the newspaper.

"Don't look at it now."

Dolan pulled his hand away.

"I'll meet you all in front of the livery stable at the end of Carlyle Street at first light," Cardwell said. "Be outfitted and ready for a one day ride."

"We'll be there," Dolan said. "When do we find out what bank we're hittin'?"

Cardwell sat back in his chair and said, "Just before we hit it."

"Why is it such a secret?" one of the other men asked.

"That's the way I do business," Cardwell said. "If you don't like it, you can bow out. I'm sure I can find somebody to take your share."

"No, no," Dolan said. "This sounds like a good deal. We don't want to give up any shares."

"Good," Cardwell said. "Then you better get started collectin' those other men."

The four men pushed back their chairs and stood up.

"And make sure they can ride, and shoot."

"Don't worry," Dolan said. "They'll be as good as us."

Cardwell had known Dolan and one of the other men—Sam Barkin—for a few years, and didn't take that as such a great recommendation. However, he needed bodies and guns, and since he planned on double-crossing every last one of them, the rest didn't really matter.

67

"I've got fifteen permanent members of the force," Police Chief Aaron Stattler said. "I can probably hire about ten more for temporary duty."

Thomas had talked and talked while the chief listened, and then was surprised when the man took everything he said at face value.

"You don't want to telegraph Vengeance Creek to confirm my story?"

"What would your motive be to warn me of an impending bank robbery?" Stattler asked.

"Maybe we're plannin' to rob one of the other banks," Cory offered.

"I consider myself a very good judge of character," the sixtyish police chief said, "and I don't think that's the case. So, let's decide how we're going to proceed."

"I guess we have to figure out which bank he's gonna hit," Cory said.

"Well," Chief Stattler said, "Bank of Denver has three branches in the city."

"Is one bigger than the others?" Thomas asked.

"I don't know if any of them is physically larger than the others," the chief said, "but I do think that one has the most money. It's in the business district, so a lot of businesses have their payrolls there."

"That's the one he'd go for, then," Thomas said, "don't you think, Ralph?"

"Seems to me if he's been workin' his way up to this bank for his whole career, he'd go for the biggest payoff. My guess is he's looking to retire."

"How many men will he have with him?" Stattler asked.

"We're not sure," Thomas said. "He used seven or eight in Vengeance Creek."

"My guess is he'd use about a dozen," Cory said.

"That would make for a big split," the chief commented.

"Actually," Thomas said, "he didn't split with anyone in his gang when he hit our bank. He left them all behind to die or get arrested while he took off with the money, and one other man. Who knows, he may have double-crossed him by now too."

"Do we have any idea when to expect them?" Stattler asked.

"We were just hopin' we'd get here before them," Thomas said. "Ralph?"

"Probably within the next few days," Cory guessed.

"Good," Stattler said, "that gives us some time to get some men together and assigned."

"Can't you send some men over now?" Thomas asked.

"It's not that easy, Deputy," the chief said. "This is a police department, and there are some protocols that need to be followed. I should be able to have some men over there by tomorrow afternoon."

"That may be too late," Thomas said.

"Better to be safe than sorry," the chief said. "I need to choose my men properly and get them into position."

"I really think you should send some men now—"

"Deputy," Stattler said, "I appreciate you bringing this to my attention, but you are very young and I believe I'm better equipped to handle this situation. Why don't you and your friend enjoy what our city has to offer for a few days while I take care of business."

Cory looked at Thomas, wondering how the deputy would handle being talked down to that way.

"You mean you don't want our help?" Thomas asked.

"You're in the big city now, Deputy," Stattler said. "This is not the old West that you're used to."

"Chief, I don't—"

"Okay, Chief," Cory said, cutting Thomas off, "we'll just be goin', then."

"Please don't misunderstand me," Stattler said,

standing. "I appreciate the information, but these things are better handled by professionals."

"What do you—"

"Let's go, Thomas," Cory said. "The chief obviously has some work to do."

Thomas wanted to stay and argue, but Cory took him by the arm and led him to the door.

Once they were outside the building, Thomas said, "I don't believe his attitude. We brought him this information. If he doesn't act quickly—"

"Thomas," Cory said, "this chief is obviously a by-the-book kind of fella. He's gonna do things at his own pace."

"And by that time Cardwell could hit the bank and be gone."

"So what do you want to do?"

Thomas eyed a café across the street and said, "Let's go over there and get somethin' to eat. I'm starvin'."

"So am I," Cory said, and they crossed over.

Once there, they both sank wearily into chairs, gave their orders to the waiter, and didn't speak again until the food was in front of them. With renewed vigor, they tore into their steaks.

"I don't know what to do, Ralph," Thomas said as he was chewing.

"Well," Cory said, "one thing we can do is telegraph your pa and tell him where we are."

"Good idea," Thomas replied. "Maybe he's even heard from James."

"Whenever Cardwell arrives, James and Berto should be right behind him."

"Unless they caught up to him," Thomas said, "and took him."

"I guess that's possible."

"You don't think so?"

"Thomas, I've been studying some of the things Ben Cardwell has done," Cory said. "I think we got to realize who we're dealin' with here."

"What are you sayin', Ralph?"

"I have an idea," Cory said, "a hunch, really. Let me lay it out for you and see what you think, okay?"

"Can we keep eatin' while you do it?"

"Definitely."

"Okay, then," Thomas said, "go ahead. . . ."

Across the street the young officer who had shown Thomas and Cory into the chief's office came into the man's office himself.

"Where'd they go?" Stattler asked him.

"They went into the café across the street, sir."

"Did you stand outside the door and listen, Peter?"

"Yes, sir," said Lieutenant Peter Masters, who acted as Stattler's personal assistant. "What are you going to do, sir?"

"We can't be at all sure they're wrong," Stattler said. "I mean, the boy's an obvious amateur."

"And the older man?"

"Not an amateur," the chief said, "but not a lawman. He seems familiar to me, as well."

"What shall we do, sir?"

"I want six men posted at the main branch of the Bank of Denver," Stattler said.

"Just that one branch, sir?"

"That's right," Stattler said, "and I want them heavily armed."

"What if they're right and the bank is hit by a dozen bank robbers, sir?"

"Six of my men should be able to handle a gang like that, Masters, don't you think?"

"Uh, yes, sir."

"Especially," Stattler added, "if they're commanded by you."

Lieutenant Masters squared his shoulders and said, "Yes, sir!"

"You choose the men," the chief said, "and have them in place by tomorrow afternoon."

"What if they hit one of the other branches, sir?"

"If this Cardwell is who I think he is, he'll hit the bank with the largest amount of deposits. I feel fairly safe in predicting that, Masters . . . don't you agree?"

The young lieutenant, who would never dream of disagreeing with his boss, said, "Yes, sir!"

"See to it, then."

Masters left, and Stattler sat back in his chair. He'd heard of Ben Cardwell, knew the man was a bank robber. If the deputy and his friend had not presented him with Cardwell's name, he would have put them down as alarmists. However, the fact that they had Cardwell's name led him to believe there was some credence to their story.

Of course, if they were wrong and he made a fool of himself by placing his men there, they'd live to regret it.

Thomas and Cory came out of the telegraph office with Thomas shaking his head.

"Why would he do that?" he asked. "Why would he leave town? Get on a horse with a wound like the one he has?"

"He was worried about you boys," Cory said. "That's why he did it."

"So now he's out there somewhere, maybe bleedin'."

"Your pa knows what he's doin'."

"I used to think so."

"What?"

Thomas was startled to realize he had said that out loud.

"Ever since Ma was killed, and Matthew, he's been different," he said. Since he'd gone ahead and started, he figured he might as well finish. "Not the same man, you know? Not as sure . . . not the same . . . father."

"You and your pa have to talk, Thomas," Cory said. "I mean, really talk."

"I know," Thomas said. "I think we've both known, but neither one of us has wanted to start."

"Well," Cory said, "somebody has to."

"You're right," Thomas said, "but after this is all over."

They started walking away from the telegraph office. The telegram from Ron Hill was in Thomas's pocket. He was not only surprised that his father had left Vengeance Creek, but that he had left it in the hands of Ron Hill.

"What do you think of my idea?" Cory asked.

"I think it's the only way for us to go," Thomas said. "It makes sense to me, especially when you said we had to consider who we were dealin' with."

"Right," Cory said. "A man who has never treated anyone fairly, a man who has probably double-crossed everyone who ever trusted him."

"It's a surprise somebody hasn't killed him by now," Thomas said.

"Well, with a little luck," Ralph Cory said, "maybe we can change that."

Thomas and Cory had each taken their own room, and that night they sat on the bed, cleaning their weapons, alone with their thoughts.

Thomas wondered where James was, and where his father was. He wondered what tomorrow or the next day would bring. He wondered if, when all was said and done, he'd actually be able to talk to his father—and have his father talk to him—so they could put aside the barrier that had been between them for the past year.

Ralph Cory wondered if Bloody Dave Macky was really gone for good. Had he ever been gone at all? With all the names he'd chosen to live under, was Ralph Cory the one that was going to stick? Or, after these weeks on the trail—back on the hunt—would he be able to go back to working in a store, or could he go back to being Dave Macky—not Bloody Dave, but just plain Dave?

While Thomas and Cory cleaned their guns and searched their minds—or their souls—Ben Cardwell led his men into Denver, after a long day's ride from Colorado Springs.

He reined his horse in and turned in his saddle to look at the rabble behind him. They stopped, except for Dolan, who rode up on him and waited for orders.

"Tell them to spread out and get lodgings for the night," Cardwell said, "and only for one night. We'll be leaving right after we hit the bank."

"Right."

"Tell them not to stay anywhere in more than twos," Cardwell went on. "I don't want anyone rememberin' us. Understand?"

"I understand."

"All right," Cardwell said.

"What about the bank?" Dolan asked. "Can you tell us where it is?"

"Sure I can," Cardwell said. "After waitin' this long, I remember exactly where it is." He gave Dolan the intersection where the largest of the Bank of Denver branches was located.

"So do we meet there?"

Cardwell nodded. "Right in front. At noon."

"We'll attract attention that way, for sure."

"We'll have the element of surprise on our side," Cardwell said. "You boys dismount, five of you come inside, six of you cover the street, watch for the law."

"And where will you be?"

"I'll already be inside the bank, waitin' for you," Cardwell said. "I'll already be there. You boys come in with your guns out, and we'll clean the bank out."

"Right." Dolan put just the right amount of enthusiasm in that one word.

Cardwell leaned over, put his hand on Dolan's shoulder and said, "This will be the biggest haul any of us has ever seen."

"Sounds good to me, Mr. Cardwell."

"Get the boys bedded down, Dolan," Cardwell said, "and I'll see you all tomorrow."

He watched as Dolan rode back to the others, gave them their instructions, and then rode off with them. He hoped they'd split up before long or else they'd attract too much attention. He just needed them to stay out of trouble until tomorrow, and then the hell with them. They'd be on their own, and so would he—with more money than he could spend in one lifetime.

69

Dolan led the gang of riders up to the front of the Bank of Denver. As agreed on, he and four others dismounted while the remaining six men remained mounted, but turned their eyes in every direction—except up.

Dolan led the others to the front door and they drew their guns. People on the street saw what was happening and scattered for cover. Dolan looked at the other men, they all nodded to each other, and he slammed the door open so they could all run into the bank.

Once inside, the six men looked around, but there was no sign of Ben Cardwell. Dolan was confused as to what to do next. While he was trying to decide, a security guard drew his gun and the bank employees hit the floor.

"Watch it!" Dolan shouted, spotting the guard, but before any of his men could do anything, four uniformed policeman stood up from behind the teller's cages and let loose with shotguns.

Outside, three policeman stood up on the roof and let loose on the six mounted bank robbers with shotguns.

When the shotguns were empty, inside and out, the policemen picked up rifles and continued to fire.

The bank robbers got off a shot or two, but the element of surprise worked against them. By the time the gunfire stopped, every last member of the gang was on the floor of the bank or on the street, good and dead.

Lieutenant Peter Masters thought that it had been incredibly easy, considering he and his men had only gotten into position a half an hour before. As usual, the chief had been right, hadn't he?

In another part of the city, Ralph Cory stood in a branch of the Bank of Denver, knowing instinctively that he was in the wrong place. He realized it was young Thomas who was going to have to face the music, because that was just the way things happened.

He was staring out the front window when a security guard sidled up beside him, hand on his gun, and asked, "Can I help you with something, sir?"

"I don't think so," Cory said. "I'm just waitin' for somebody."

"I see," the guard said. "Well . . . I'll just keep an eye out."

"You do that," Cory said. "After all, it's your job, isn't it?"

"Yes, sir," the guard said. "It is."

Ben Cardwell rode up to the front of the bank and dismounted nonchalantly. About now the rest of the gang were getting themselves shot to hell, or maybe they were holding the bank up without him. Either way, didn't matter to him. They could keep whatever money—or lead—they collected. This was the bank he wanted. It didn't have the largest deposits, but it had enough to last one man a long time.

He looked up and down the street, on the lookout for any sign of a policeman. He didn't expect to see any, but if he did, he would have called the whole thing off. Whatever was happening at the other branch, it must have been holding the attention of most of the police in Denver by now.

Satisfied that he was in the clear, he opened the door of the bank and entered. It had one security guard, who gave him a bored look. He wouldn't be a problem.

There were a couple of customers at the tellers' windows, and some other employees sitting at desks. The only one he had to worry about was the guard, and he figured the element of surprise should take care of that.

He waited, pretending to fill out a deposit slip,

or a withdrawal slip, while the customers finished their business and left. The guard's back was turned, and the moment was right.

He started to approach the guard when a door slammed open—the door to the manager's office—and Thomas Shaye stepped out. . . .

Thomas wanted to wait longer, but knew he couldn't afford to. He didn't know what Cardwell meant to do to the guard, knock him out or shoot him in the back. He couldn't take the chance.

He hadn't tried to convince the people in the bank that a robbery might take place. If everybody had believed him and left, Cardwell would have been suspicious when he walked in. Everything had to look normal.

He had, however, gotten the bank manager to agree to let him stay in the office.

"One day," the man said, "that's all I can give you. I'll be checking in with the chief of police at the end of the day."

"You do that," Thomas said. He had a feeling they'd gotten to Denver just ahead of Cardwell, anyway. "I'll take the one day."

And that had been all it had taken, after all. . . .

Thomas stepped out of the manager's office quickly and shouted, "Cardwell!"

The bank robber holding his gun stopped, and the guard turned quickly, going for his own gun.

With his bare hand, Cardwell hit the man quickly, just once, knocking him out.

"Are you one of the deputies?" Cardwell asked, his back to Thomas, as the bank employees dropped to the floor.

"That's right," Thomas said. "From Vengeance Creek."

"You tracked me all the way here?"

"Got here ahead of you, actually." Somebody moved, and Thomas shouted, "Everybody stay down!"

"That's good advice!" Cardwell added holding his gun up in one hand. "Listen to the deputy." Then, still turned away from Thomas, he said, "You alone, Deputy?"

"I am," Thomas said. "There's another, but he's at one of the other branches."

"I see," Cardwell said. "And the large branch?"

"The police are there."

"That's good," Cardwell said, "very good. In fact, that works out perfectly."

"Set up some more men to be killed, did you?"

"Of course," Cardwell said. "That's my style, isn't it? I don't like to share."

"Not somethin' to brag about, if you ask me."

"Okay, Deputy," Cardwell said, "I'm gonna turn around now, and we can get this settled so I can get to work."

"You're not robbin' this bank, Cardwell," Thomas said, "or any other ever again."

"Well, we'll see," Cardwell said. "I'm gonna

turn around now, unless you want to shoot me in the back?"

"It's what you deserve."

"But you won't do it, will you? So I'll just turn around with my hands in the air . . . don't get nervous, lad. . . ."

Cardwell did a slow turn while the other people in the bank kept their noses to the floor. When he saw that Thomas's gun was holstered, he laughed and lowered his hands.

"Not a good move, boy," the bank robber said.

"I'm takin' you in," Thomas said.

"No, I don't think so, Deputy," Cardwell said, loosely holding the gun in one hand. "I'm gonna kill you, and then take as much money out of this bank as I can carry."

"And are you gonna kill everyone who works here too, Cardwell?" Thomas asked. "Like you did in Vengeance Creek?"

"Who knows?" Cardwell said. "I might be in a really good mood after I kill you."

"The easiest thing would be for you to give up," Thomas said.

"You know," Cardwell said, "I'd ask you where your father and brother are, but I really don't have the time . . . and I don't care. I'm kind of impressed that you came all this way . . ."

"Don't be."

". . . to die."

Cardwell lifted the gun, but Thomas saw the man's muscles tense just a split second before. He snatched his own gun from his holster and fired once, hitting Cardwell in the chest before he could fire.

Thomas walked to the fallen man, took his gun from his hand, and tossed it away, just to be on the safe side, but the bank robber was dead.

"Not in such a good mood, after all?" Thomas asked. "Are you?"

EPILOGUE

Telegrams came and went, and three days after Thomas had killed Ben Cardwell, he and Ralph Cory rode into the town of Trinidad. Waiting for them in the dining room at the Columbian Hotel were both Dan and James Shaye, and Rigoberto Colon. They all exchanged information to fill in the gaps. . . .

At the home of Wendy Williams, earlier in the week, Dan Shaye had received a telegram from Vengeance Creek. Ron Hill had told him that he had gotten a telegram from Trinidad that James was being held by the law there until his identity could be confirmed. Shaye had taken his newly bandaged wound onto a horse and set out for Trinidad, still not knowing where Thomas was.

"He let me stay in jail until he got here," James complained to Thomas, "me and Berto both."

"I told you," Shaye said, "the sheriff wouldn't

take my word in a telegram. I had to come here and identify myself."

"Why would he take your word that you're the sheriff of Vengeance Creek?" James asked. "And not take my word that I was a deputy?"

"You'll have to ask him that," Shaye said.

After Cardwell's death the chief of police of Denver had taken the credit in the newspaper for foiling not one bank robbery, but two. He did so without acknowledging Thomas's part at all. Thomas didn't care, though. By exchanging telegrams with Ron Hill in Vengeance Creek, he discovered that his father was going to Trinidad to get James out of jail. He and Cory immediately set out for that town.

"I'm kind of sorry they let you out before I got here," Thomas said across the table to his brother. "That would have been funny to see."

"Ha, ha," James said. "Me and Berto didn't think it was very funny, and him with a bullet wound in his shoulder."

"How are you, by the way?" Dan Shaye asked Colon.

"Better, *Jefe*," Colon said. "Actually, the time allowed me to rest, and heal."

"Speaking of healin'," Thomas said to his father, "you shouldn't be on a horse yet, should you?"

"Well, if one of you four had thought to send

me a telegram," Shaye sad, "I would have known where you were."

"Sorry, Pa . . ." James said.

"*Sí,*" Colon said, "sorry, *Jefe.*"

"So what happened with the other man?" Cory asked. "Jacks, was it?"

Shaye looked at James, who told Cory and Thomas what had happened when he and Colon had ridden into Trinidad that first day.

"Good for you, James," Thomas said. "You took him."

"It was just . . . instinct," James said. "I didn't even realize what was happenin' until after I fired."

"That's the way it happens sometimes, James," Shaye said.

"Maybe you were born for this after all, James," Thomas said.

Yes, Shaye thought, maybe he was . . . in fact, maybe both his sons were.

Thomas gave a brief recount of what happened in Denver, bringing his brother and father up to date.

"Well," Ralph Cory said, "coincidence seems to have had a lot to do with bringin' this all to a satisfactory end. James and Berto ridin' in just as Jacks was gettin' in a shootout; Thomas and me gettin' to Denver just a day ahead of Cardwell."

"Maybe not so much coincidence," Shaye said, "as hard work and determination."

"I'll drink to that," Thomas said, raising his coffee cup.

"So it's over," James said.

"It's over," Shaye said.

"I'll drink to that," Cory said, and lifted his own cup, followed by the others.

"What do we do now, Pa?" James asked.

"We get one night in this fine hotel," Shaye said, "and then we head home."

Nobody said a word.

"Ralph?" he said. "You are goin' back to Vengeance Creek, aren't you?"

"I don't think so, Sheriff," Cory said. "I think I just may . . . oh, hit the trail for a while. I don't think I want to get back behind a store counter just yet."

"Well," Shaye said, "good luck to you, then. Berto? You comin' back?"

Rigoberto Colon frowned and said, "It is a very long way to go back, *Jefe*. Perhaps, if Señor Ralph doesn't mind, I will ride with him for a while."

That brought the attention back to Cory.

"Hell, I don't mind," Cory said, "except that I think we both make lousy coffee."

"I will chance it," Colon said, "if you will, señor."

"Sure, why not?" Cory looked at the three Shayes. "I guess you boys'll be ridin' back to Vengeance Creek without us. At least you've got your jobs waitin' for you there."

"Well," Shaye said, "I've been thinkin' about that."

"About what, Pa?" James asked.

"Our jobs," Shaye said. "I think I'm about done bein' the sheriff of Vengeance Creek."

"Are we done bein' lawmen, Pa?" James asked.

"I don't know, James," Shaye said. "I guess that'll be up to each of us to decide when we get back there."

"Why go back at all?" Cory asked.

"We've got to tie up some loose ends," Shaye said, "and bring back the bank's money,"

"Ah," Cory said, "loose ends. Life seems full of them, doesn't it?"

"Speakin' of which," Shaye said, "who's Berto gonna be ridin' with, Ralph Cory or Dave Macky?"

"I think it might be time for Dave Macky to put in an appearance, again," Cory/Macky replied. "In fact, I was thinkin' of hittin' the trail right away, nice as a night in this hotel sounds. Berto? Can you ride?"

"*Sí*, Señor Ralph—I mean, Señor Dave." The Mexican stood up. "I can ride."

"Gents," Macky said. "Good luck to you."

"And you," Shaye said.

The men shook hands all around, and then Macky turned to Thomas.

"Good luck, Thomas," he said. "It was a pleasure ridin' with you."

"You too . . . Dave. It was a privilege."

Macky and Colon waved one last time and left the hotel, leaving the three Shaye men at the table, alone.

"Pa?" Thomas said.

"Yes, Thomas?"

"There's somethin' I been meanin' to talk to you about for a long time."

"Really?" Shaye asked. "Well, there's another coincidence for you. There's somethin' I been meanin' to talk to you about too."

James sat back and listened to his brother and father clear the air, hoping that maybe some of the ghosts from the year gone by might soon be gone . . . or at least laid to rest.

ACTION-PACKED *LAW FOR HIRE* ADVENTURES BY

BILL BROOKS

PROTECTING HICKOK

0-06-054176-8/$5.99 US/$7.99 Can

Determined to hunt down his brother's killer, city-bred
Teddy Blue joins the Pinkerton Detective Agency. But Teddy
gets more than he bargained for in the wide open West, when he's
assigned as a bodyguard to the famous "Wild Bill" Hickok.

DEFENDING CODY

0-06-054177-6/$5.99 US/$7.99 Can

When he's hired as professional protection for "Buffalo Bill" Cody
out in the wild, Teddy's caught in a deadly tangle that may
prove too much for one hired guardian to handle.

SAVING MASTERSON

0-06-054178-4/$5.99 US/$7.99 Can

It's just Teddy Blue and lawman Bat Masterson against
pretty much the whole damn town of Dodge City . . .
with the killers lining up to take their shots.

AuthorTracker

Don't miss the next book by your favorite author.
Sign up now for AuthorTracker by visiting
www.AuthorTracker.com

Available wherever books are sold
or please call 1-800-331-3761 to order.

LFH 0304

SEALS

THE WARRIOR BREED

by H. Jay Riker

THE BEST OF THE BEST, AT SEA, IN THE AIR, AND ON LAND

SILVER STAR
0-380-76967-0/$6.99 US/$8.99 Can

PURPLE HEART
0-380-76969-7/$6.99 US/$9.99 Can

BRONZE STAR
0-380-76970-0/$6.99 US/$9.99 Can

NAVY CROSS
0-380-78555-2/$5.99 US/$7.99 Can

MEDAL OF HONOR
0-380-78556-0/$7.99 US/$10.99 Can

MARKS OF VALOR
0-380-78557-9/$6.99 US/$9.99 Can

IN HARM'S WAY
0-380-79507-8/$7.99 US/$10.99 Can

DUTY'S CALL
0-380-79508-6/$6.99 US/$9.99 Can

CASUALTIES OF WAR
0-380-79510-8/$6.99 US/$9.99 Can

AuthorTracker
www.AuthorTracker.com

Available wherever books are sold or please call 1-800-331-3761 to order.

SEA 1204

DON'T MISS ANY OF THE THRILLING
SHARPSHOOTER
WESTERN ADVENTURES FROM
TOBIAS COLE

One man with a duty to the dead, and a lethal talent honed by war . . .

THE
SHARPSHOOTER
REPENTANCE CREEK
0-06-053533-4/$5.99 US/$7.99 Can

THE
SHARPSHOOTER
GOLD FEVER
0-06-053530-X/$5.99 US/$7.99 Can

THE
SHARPSHOOTER
BRIMSTONE
0-06-053529-6/$5.99 US/$7.99 Can

www.AuthorTracker.com

Available wherever books are sold
or please call 1-800-331-3761 to order.

SHS 1204

EXPLOSIVE UNDERSEA ACTION

H. JAY RIKER's

THE SILENT SERVICE

GRAYBACK CLASS
0-380-80466-2 • $6.99 US • $9.99 Can

The year is 1985 and reports have been received of a devastating new Soviet weapon, a prototype attack submarine more advanced than anything in the U.S undersea arsenal.

LOS ANGELES CLASS
0-380-80467-0 • $6.99 US • $9.99 Can

In 1987 a hand-picked team of SEALs will venture into the deadly, Russian-patrolled seas off the coast of the Kamchatka Peninsula to stop an enemy spy from leading a boat full of brave men to their doom.

SEAWOLF CLASS
0-380-80468-9 • $6.99 US • $9.99 Can

In the chaos of the first major conflict of the twenty-first century, the People's Republic of China sets out to "reclaim" by force the territories it considers its own: the Spratly Islands in the South China Sea . . . and Taiwan.

VIRGINIA CLASS
0-06-052438-3 • $6.99 US • $9.99 Can

A rogue Kilo-class submarine built by a shadowy and powerful ally has become the latest weapon in al Qaeda's terrorist arsenal. The sub's brutal strikes have created an explosive hostage situation in the Pacific . . . and have left hundreds dead.

Available wherever books are sold or please call 1-800-331-3761 to order.

 AuthorTracker
www.AuthorTracker.com

SIL 0504

BLAZING WESTERN FICTION FROM MASTER STORYTELLER

BILL DUGAN

BRADY'S LAW
0-06-100628-9/$5.99 US/$7.99 Can

Dan Brady is a man who believes in truth—and in a justice
he won't get from the law.

TEXAS DRIVE
0-06-100032-9/$5.99 US/$7.99 Can

Ted Cotton can no longer avoid the kind of bloody violence
that sickened him during the War Between the States.

GUN PLAY AT CROSS CREEK
0-06-100079-5/$5.99 US/$7.99 Can

Morgan Atwater's got one final score to settle.

DUEL ON THE MESA
0-06-100033-7/$5.99 US/$7.99 Can

Together Dalton Chance and Lone Wolf blaze a trail
of deadly vengeance.

MADIGAN'S LUCK
0-06-100677-7/$5.99 US/$7.99 Can

One successful drive across the open range can change
Dave Madigan's luck from bad to good.

 AuthorTracker
www.AuthorTracker.com

Available wherever books are sold
or please call 1-800-331-3761 to order.

DUG 0604

Now Available from HarperTorch, Classic Westerns from the *New York Times* Bestselling Author

Elmore Leonard

"As welcome as a thunderstorm in a dry spell."
Dallas Morning News

← →

VALDEZ IS COMING
0-380-82223-7/$5.99 US/$7.99 Can

HOMBRE
0-380-82224-5/$5.99 US/$7.99 Can

THE BOUNTY HUNTERS
0-380-82225-3/$5.99 US/$7.99 Can

ESCAPE FROM FIVE SHADOWS
0-06-001348-6/$5.99 US/$7.99 Can

THE LAW AT RANDADO
0-06-001349-4/$5.99 US/$7.99 Can

GUNSIGHTS
0-06-001350-8/$5.99 US/$7.99 Can

FORTY LASHES LESS ONE
0-380-82233-4/$5.99 US/$7.99 Can

LAST STAND AT SABER RIVER
0-06-001352-4$/5.99 US/$7.99 Can

AuthorTracker
www.AuthorTracker.com

Available wherever books are sold
or please call 1-800-331-3761 to order.

ELW 0604